"Nice to meet you, Heather Fitzpatrick. I'm Jim Dyer,"

said the stranger trapped in the elevator with her. He flashed an honest-to-God dimple as he smiled.

Heather eyed his broad shoulders and impressive biceps, telling herself that a pregnant woman had no business staring at a good-looking man that way. Still, if she let herself, she might just forget that she was trapped in an elevator, the pains in her midsection getting worse by the minute.

She jerked with a sudden pang and felt the color drain from her face.

Jim stared at her. "What's wrong?" He gazed into her widening eyes. "Heather?"

She wet her lips and tried to smile. "I hate to impose on our very short acquaintance…" she began. "But I think I'm about to deliver my baby!"

Dear Reader,

Welcome to Special Edition…where each month we offer six wonderfully emotional romances about people just like you—striving to find the perfect balance between life, career, family and, of course, love.…

To start off, Susan Mallery shines with her thirtieth Silhouette novel, *Surprise Delivery*. In this not-to-be-missed THAT'S MY BABY! title, a very pregnant heroine is stuck in an elevator with a charming stranger—and is about to give birth!

Love proves to be the greatest adventure of all in *Hunter's Pride* by Lindsay McKenna. In the continuation of her enthralling MORGAN'S MERCENARIES: THE HUNTERS series, fiercely proud Devlin Hunter is teamed up with a feisty beauty who challenges him at every turn. And don't miss the wonderful romance between a harried single dad and a spirited virgin in *The Home Love Built* by Christine Flynn.

Next, a compassionate paralegal reunites a brooding cop with his twin sons in *The Fatherhood Factor*—book three in Diana Whitney's heartwarming FOR THE CHILDREN series. Then a lovely newcomer befriends her neighbor's little boy and breaks through to the lad's guarded dad in *My Child, Our Child* by *New York Times* bestselling author Patricia Hagan.

Finally this month, Tracy Sinclair pens *The Bachelor King,* a regally romantic tale about a powerful king who marries a "pregnant" American beauty, only to receive the royal shock of his life!

I hope you enjoy these six unforgettable romances created *by* women like you, *for* women like you!

Sincerely,

Karen Taylor Richman
Senior Editor

Please address questions and book requests to:
Silhouette Reader Service
U.S.: 3010 Walden Ave., P.O. Box 1325, Buffalo, NY 14269
Canadian: P.O. Box 609, Fort Erie, Ont. L2A 5X3

SUSAN MALLERY

SURPRISE DELIVERY

SPECIAL EDITION®

Published by Silhouette Books

America's Publisher of Contemporary Romance

To my mother, with love

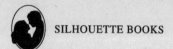

SILHOUETTE BOOKS

ISBN 0-373-24273-5

SURPRISE DELIVERY

Copyright © 1999 by Susan W. Macias

Visit us at www.romance.net

Printed in U.S.A.

Books by Susan Mallery

SUSAN MALLERY

was thrilled when she realized that *Surprise Delivery* was her thirtieth romance for Harlequin and Silhouette Books. For her, writing romances—books that affirm the choices of the heart—is a dream come true. She's a favorite with readers. Her books frequently appear on many bestseller lists and she's promised that she'll do her best to write at least thirty more wonderful romances.

Dear Reader,

There's something wonderful about a man who likes kids—and babies. We'll forgive him almost anything, mostly because if he has that much heart and that much patience, he can't be all bad. Besides, the sight of a big, strong macho guy going all cuddly with a tiny baby in his arms makes even the toughest female melt.

Unfortunately, Heather Fitzpatrick, my heroine, has sworn off men. She's a firm believer in the three-strikes rule, and she's had three huge strikeouts in the romance department. So when she finds herself about to be a single mom, she's determined to make it on her own. She's smart, she's prepared, she's going to give birth in an elevator.

What? Yeah, it's kind of funny, really. Heather's doctor swears she's not going to go into labor for another few days. So that very afternoon, when Heather's elevator car gets stuck between floors and her water breaks, she tells herself not to panic. Which is a good thing, because handsome, strong, single Jim Dyer is panicking enough for both of them. Although he's not about to let it show. When push comes to shove (if you'll excuse the pun), he rolls up his sleeves and delivers Heather's beautiful daughter into the world.

Surprisingly enough, he turns out to be one of those guys who adores children, and babies in particular. And Heather finds it mighty hard to resist the sight of him going all cuddly with her little girl.

Maybe, just maybe, she's going to get one more chance at love. And maybe Jim is going to find the family he's always wanted.

Enjoy!

Susan Mallery

Chapter One

"Please hold the elevator," Heather Fitzpatrick called as she made a sincere but futile attempt to hurry toward the open doors. She was nearly out of breath as she stepped inside. "Thanks," she said with a smile as she glanced at the man pressing the door open button. "I'm not completely sure these are the slowest elevators in the eleven Western states, but I think they're in the top ten." She rubbed the small of her back, trying to ease an ache that had settled there about three months ago and had yet to disappear. "I couldn't bear the thought of waiting ten minutes for the elevator to come back up to this floor."

"I'll bet," the man said, unable to take his gaze from her midsection.

By now Heather was used to men looking at her with expressions that bordered on panic. While *he* was tall, dark-haired and handsome, *she* was a walking belly with stick arms and legs. "I know what you're thinking," she said, resting her hand on the top of her stomach and leaning against the wall of the elevator. "It looks worse than it is. According to my doctor, I have nearly a week until I pop or give birth, whichever comes first. I'm sure you'll be safe for the short ride down to the parking level."

"Promise?" he asked, his voice low and teasing.

"No, but my doctor swears it's true," she told him. "I just saw her, and despite my pleas to the contrary, she's sentenced me to several more days of incubating."

"Sounds painful."

"I'm ready for it to be over, but not just because I'm tired of being pregnant—" Heather rubbed her abdomen "—I'm anxious to meet my baby."

The elevator doors crawled closed, creaking all the way. After a couple of seconds, the car started a painfully slow descent. Heather told herself to keep breathing. She normally didn't notice time spent in an elevator, but her pregnancy and the hormones it produced had made her claustrophobic. As if swollen ankles and stretch marks weren't enough.

She watched the light come on for the third floor, then the second. She waited for the light indicating they'd passed the first floor and were on their way to the parking garage. Instead, the elevator suddenly stopped.

Her breath caught in her throat. The man pushed the door open button. Nothing happened.

"We're stuck," Heather said, trying not to panic.

"Maybe not," the man told her. He pushed the

button for the parking level again, then the door open button.

Heather felt her chest tightening. She was going to scream. She knew in her head that getting upset wouldn't help, but she couldn't stop herself. She wanted to beat her fists against the side of the car and demand that someone let her out.

"You okay?" the man asked as he glanced up from the panel he'd been studying.

"Never better."

One corner of his mouth twitched. "You're not a good liar."

"I always meant to be," Heather said, trying to distract herself with conversation. "You know how it goes. As a child, one aspires to lie well, but there's that whole honesty-is-the-best-policy thing, and somehow, I just couldn't make it happen."

He grinned. "As long as you have a goal. I'll make you a deal. I'll get us out of here if you won't panic."

"Sounds great. I'm perfectly calm, so you can go ahead and open the doors now."

"Give me a second." He picked up the phone under the control panel and waited. "Yeah, we're stuck in an elevator." He paused and listened. "If you're facing the elevators, we're in the one on the right." Another pause. "Okay, we'll sit tight. There are two of us and we're fine." He glanced at Heather. "Are you still fine?"

She nodded. She wasn't really, but he undoubtedly didn't want to hear about her fears or her urge to break down the doors.

He hung up the phone and faced her. "They think one of the fuses blew and the motor automatically shut down. Normally, it would take us to the ground floor, but this time it didn't. So we're going to be here for a few minutes while they get a new fuse and reset the controls.''

Heather eyed him. She wasn't the only one who was a bad liar. He wouldn't look directly at her.

"What aren't you telling me?'' she asked.

"Nothing.'' He shoved his hands in his back pockets but still wouldn't meet her gaze.

"Uh-huh. That's like me saying I'm only a little bit pregnant. Come on. What did the guy say?''

Blue eyes finally looked at her face. "It'll take close to an hour.''

"Are we at risk of falling?''

"No. We're perfectly safe, but it's gonna be a little while.''

She exhaled and felt some of her tension ease. "I think I can survive that.''

"You sure?''

He looked concerned. Heather allowed herself to savor the feeling, wondering when was the last time someone had worried about her. Her doctor wanted to make sure she was eating right and taking her vitamins. She had some friends at work who asked after her, her mother cared, but no one really worried.

"I swear, I'm fine.'' She glanced around. "But I do need to sit down.'' Logically, she knew the floor was as far away as it had been ever since she'd stopped growing at thirteen. But as her girth increased, floors had seemed farther and farther away. And currently she felt as ungainly as a cow in mud.

The man took a step toward her. "How can I help?''

She held out her hand. "If you could just help me lower myself, that would be great."

He grasped her hands firmly. She liked the feel of his strong fingers and the way he didn't make a big deal out of her request. Bracing herself, she slid against the wall of the elevator, letting him slow her until she was finally sitting down. Her cotton maternity dress billowed out around her and her skinny legs stuck out in front. She was incredibly out of proportion. Sometimes she felt like a cartoon character.

"I'm Jim Dyer," the man said as he sat down across from her.

"Heather Fitzpatrick."

"Nice to meet you, Heather."

He flashed her a dimple as he smiled. She'd never actually met a man with an honest-to-God dimple before. It was nice, as were his blue eyes and the man himself. His relaxed and comfortable manner made her feel better about the whole situation. If she let herself, she just might forget that she was trapped in an elevator.

Uh-oh. It had been a mistake to think the "e" word.

There was a brief pause. Heather felt her anxiety growing, so she searched for a neutral topic of conversation. Anything to distract herself from her tension, not to mention the steady pressure against her back. The pain moved around her abdomen, but she figured that was just her uncomfortable position sitting on the floor.

"What do you do?" she asked.

"I own a helicopter charter company," he said.

"At the Van Nuys airport. I'm here getting my yearly physical so I can stay certified to fly."

She eyed his broad shoulders and the healthy color in his face. He wore a long-sleeved shirt tucked into khaki slacks, and worn boots. Like most other living, breathing women, she could appreciate a man who had a well-proportioned body. In her present oversize condition, she was even more aware of how nice it was to be normal.

She ripped her gaze away from his impressive biceps, told herself that a pregnant woman had no business staring at a good-looking man and tried to think of something clever to say.

Clever eluded her, so she settled on obvious. "You fly helicopters?"

"It comes with the business. I have pilots, but occasionally I do a run myself."

"I don't think I've ever been up in one."

"Do you like to fly?"

She thought of her lone trip to Florida to visit her mother. "'Like' is a strong term. I don't mind it."

"Commercial flying is different from a helicopter. You're removed from the experience and you can't see anything."

"You make that sound bad."

"Isn't it?"

"I don't think so."

"Tell you what. When you've had your baby and you're feeling better, come on out to the airport and I'll give you a sight-seeing tour of the valley. Everything looks better from up there."

"That's so nice. In return I could let you change a diaper or two."

"Ouch. Okay, point taken. You don't have to fly in a helicopter if you don't want to."

"Gee, thanks." She smiled, then shifted on the hard floor. The pain in her back was getting worse by the minute. All she wanted was to crawl into her own bed, but even that didn't bring much relief these days. It wasn't just that she felt as if she'd swallowed a basketball; it was that someone kept pumping the sucker bigger and bigger.

"What about you?" Jim asked. "What do you do? Or should I say *did* you do?"

"Oh, I'm still working," Heather told him. "I do assembly in a factory in the West Valley." She wrinkled her nose. "I know it's not glamorous, but the benefits are great and I've been getting bonus pay for working the swing shift. No one likes that one because you lose your evenings. I plan to work up to the very last day so I can have a longer paid maternity leave."

She thought about having to report to her job later that evening and nearly groaned out loud. The burst of energy that had sustained her for the past few days had faded. She shifted again as the pain moved lower, from her belly into her legs.

"I also have a home bookkeeping business," Heather continued. "I've been going to college part-time. I'm just two classes shy of my bachelor's degree in accounting, so I'm able to do books for small businesses."

She rubbed her belly. "The timing of my pregnancy is great. I have savings and the pay from my maternity leave. Between that and my business, I probably won't have to go back to the factory job for at least a year, which means I can be home with my baby. In the meantime, I'll look for something in bookkeeping. While factory work pays the bills, it isn't the most interesting job on the planet.'' She covered her mouth with her fingers. ''Sorry, I'm telling you way more than you wanted to know.''

''No, I'm enjoying hearing about your plans.''

At five feet seven inches, Heather was fairly tall for a woman, but Jim dwarfed her. Even sitting down, he looked big and strong.

''It sounds like you work a lot of hours. Is that okay?'' He tilted his head slightly to indicate her stomach.

''Yes. I'm very healthy.''

He didn't look convinced. ''Even so, your long days must make your husband worry about you.''

She resisted the urge to stick her finger down her throat and make gagging noises. ''I'm not married, so that's not a problem.''

''Oh.'' Jim looked a little embarrassed. ''Well, the father of your baby, then.''

Heather leaned her head against the wall of the elevator and closed her eyes. ''The father of my baby is a no-good rat,'' she said, her voice calm. ''And I'm a fool.'' She opened her eyes and shrugged. ''He told me he was divorced and I believed him. Even when he seemed to 'travel' all the time.''

''He was lying?''

''With every single word. It turned out that he and his wife were just separated. While he was seeing me, he was considering a reconciliation with his wife. Not that he ever told me.''

Heather tried to force those thoughts from her

mind. There was no point in rehashing the past. Luke had been a low spot in her life, but she'd gotten over him. The good news was that she was about to have a baby and she'd always wanted children. As her mother used to tell her, even the darkest cloud had a silver lining.

"He was seeing both of you at the same time?" Jim asked, outraged.

She'd forgotten there were still a few good men left on the planet. "Imagine how *I* felt," she said. "The day I told him I was pregnant, he left me to return to her. It turns out she was pregnant, too." Heather realized what she'd said and pressed her lips together. "This is crazy. I've just told you something incredibly personal and I don't even know you. I'm really sorry. I don't usually babble like this. It must be the hormones."

"No. It's the elevator. I've heard they have this effect on people."

"It must only be on women," she grumbled. "I don't hear you spilling your guts."

"I don't have anything interesting to share, otherwise I would."

"Maybe you could make up something. You know, just to make me feel better."

He thought for a moment. "How about if I confess that I used to be a woman?"

Heather smiled. She eyed his long, lean frame and the masculine shape of his head. "Not likely. Is that the best you can come up with?"

"Sorry, yes."

They both laughed.

"I could beat him up for you," Jim suddenly said.

Not sure she'd understood the statement, Heather blinked, then had to figure out who the "him" was. "Luke?"

"The father of your baby. I'm assuming if he went back to his wife, he's not interested in his kid."

She nodded slowly. Luke had warned her he was going to deny paternity. "He doesn't want his wife to know about the affair," she admitted. "Acknowledging the baby would mean telling her the truth. I decided that rather than having someone with his defective character around my child, I would prefer that he never know him or her." She touched her belly in a protective gesture. "We had a lawyer draw up the paperwork. He signed away his rights to the child, and I agreed to never contact him or pursue child support."

Jim made a low sound in his throat. "Like I said, the guy needs a good beating."

She stared at him for a long time without speaking. He was incredibly good-looking and, from what she could tell during their brief acquaintance, a real, live hero. "Do you walk old ladies across the street in your spare time?" she asked.

"No. But I do think a man should always do the right thing. You're in no position to teach this guy a lesson, so I'm volunteering. I don't mind helping."

He wasn't kidding. Heather didn't know what to do with that information. She couldn't remember the last time she'd met a decent man, at least not one under the age of fifty.

"You're a nice man, Jim Dyer," she said. "I know that men hate to be called nice because it's not macho and sexy, however I'm hoping you'll indulge me and simply accept my compliment. I mean it most sincerely.''

"Thank you.''

She sighed softly. How would her life have been different if she'd met someone like him during the past ten years instead of the three deadbeats she'd been involved with? Heather shrugged off the thought. She didn't believe in dwelling on the past or the difficult times in her life. Right now, she was doing great. She was healthy, about to give birth, and financially she was going to be fine. She had everything she needed. If a dream or two was going unfulfilled, so what? It wouldn't be the first time that had happened.

"What are you thinking?" Jim asked.

"That I'm very lucky.''

"Because you're trapped in an elevator with me?"

His eyes were an impossible shade of blue—dark and welcoming, not to mention fringed with long lashes.

"Compared with some of the other possibilities, you are the ideal elevator companion," she said. "You don't seem the type to start panicking, which is good. One of us should remain calm and in control.''

"You're doing great," he said. "I can barely notice you're nervous.''

"Gee, thanks.''

But she didn't mind his teasing. He was easy to talk to, concerned without being intrusive, but strong. If he were—

Pain ripped through Heather. She felt as if invisible hands were twisting her in two from the inside out.

She was so stunned by the sensation she couldn't breathe, couldn't even cry out. Then it was gone and she was left to wonder what on earth was happening to her.

Jim glanced at the phone in the elevator panel and thought about calling to find out how much longer the repair would take. So far, Heather was holding up great, but the stress of being trapped in an elevator couldn't be good for her. She had a pretty face, with big green eyes and a mouth that smiled easily. She looked as if she should have given birth a month ago. With her arms and legs so thin, she looked all tummy and very uncomfortable.

His gaze drifted to her stomach and he tried to imagine the baby inside. He didn't want to think about children or infants, but it was hard not to. So he forced himself to concentrate specifically on Heather and not to think about his past.

Heather was bright, funny and pregnant. What kind of bastard would turn his back on her? He shook his head slightly and told himself she was better off without the jerk in her life. He wondered if she felt the same way. She'd sounded as if she was more than ready to write off the guy, but women didn't always—

Heather jerked suddenly. Jim stared at her. ''What's wrong?''

Color drained from her face. Her knees came up toward her chest and her hands curled into fists. Even before she spoke, he saw the pool of water darkening the gray carpet on the floor of the elevator.

''Heather?''

Her eyes were big and unfocused. She wet her lips and tried to smile. ''I hate to impose on our very short acquaintance, but I think I'm going to have this baby. Now!''

Chapter Two

"You're kidding, right?" Jim asked desperately, not wanting to believe what he'd heard. This couldn't be happening. Not to either of them. He did *not* want to be trapped in an elevator with a woman about to give birth, and he knew she wanted to be stuck with him even less.

The damp stain on the carpet grew as another fierce contraction gripped her. Heather blanched as she squeezed her eyes closed and gasped for breath.

"I'm sorry," she said when the pain faded. She looked at him and tried to smile. "I wish I was kidding, but as you can probably tell, my water broke, and from the pain, I'm assuming this is the real thing."

Her face was thin and pale, just like her arms and legs. She wore a short-sleeved green dress that billowed out around her, making her look like a small child dressed up in her mother's clothing. Except there was nothing childlike about her discomfort or her large belly.

Jim swore silently, wondering what the hell he was supposed to do. All he wanted was to walk away. He shifted uneasily. "Are you all right?" he asked awkwardly, then waved his hand. "Stupid question. Don't bother answering it."

"And here I promised you I wouldn't go into labor before reaching the parking level."

Her words were light, as was her tone, but he saw the fear lurking in her green eyes. She rubbed her forehead; the action left her bangs mussed and spiky. Her hair was the color of corn silk and fell past her shoulders. She wore it tied back in a ribbon. He'd noticed that completely feminine adornment the minute she'd walked into the elevator. He hadn't known that women still wore ribbons in their hair.

"I don't suppose that in addition to flying helicopters you have a weekend hobby of delivering babies?" she asked.

She was half teasing, half hoping. He read the truth in her pinched face. He was all she had. If nothing else, he had to make her believe everything would be all right. He moved across the small space and crouched beside her. Perspiration dotted her forehead and her upper lip. Her eyes were wide, her mouth trembling. He wanted to make her feel better, but there was little he could do except reassure her.

"No training at delivering babies, but I'm a real quick study." He took her hand in his and squeezed. "You have my complete attention, Heather." He gave her a quick smile. "You don't know me from a rock, but I promise that I'm great in a crisis. Together we'll get through this. Okay?"

She nodded. "Do you mind if I scream?"

"Do you need to?"

"Not right now, but I might later."

"Then go for it." He gave her fingers another squeeze to reassure her, then reached for the phone. "I'm going to check on their progress. With a little luck, they'll get the elevator fixed long before you're ready to have your baby."

"I'm sure I don't have to tell you to ask them to hurry," she said, then folded in on herself with a wave of pain.

Jim forced himself to look calm. He'd had a little bit of first-aid training when he'd been in the navy, but none of his classes had dealt with childbirth. Sure, he'd seen it on television, but he had a feeling that the programs hadn't been totally forthcoming about all that took place during a delivery.

He swore silently as he picked up the phone. The line connected instantly with the maintenance room. A man answered.

"I know," he began hastily. "You two are ready to get out of there, but it's going to be a little bit longer. It's not the fuse like we first thought. That number two elevator is a temperamental girl, and we don't want to rush this."

"I don't give a damn what kind of problems you're having," Jim said, his voice low. "The woman with me has gone into labor. She's in a lot of pain, and we need to get her to a hospital before she has her baby right here."

There was a moment of silence on the other end of the line, followed by an explosion of cursing. Jim held the phone away from his ear.

Heather smiled. "Wow. You got his attention."

"Are you surprised?"

She shook her head. "I just hope he can do something."

Jim did, too. Heather had shifted herself into the corner of the elevator. Her feet were flat on the carpet, so she could brace herself against the wall. He didn't want to think for what. Weren't first babies always late and very slow in coming? He could only hope that was true and that this would prove to be one of those long, drawn-out labors. Not that he wanted Heather to be in pain, but there was no way he could deliver her child.

"Okay," the maintenance guy said into the phone. "We're going to try a couple of things to get the elevator down to the ground floor so that we can pry open the doors. In the meantime, we're calling an ambulance. How's she doing?"

"I don't know," Jim said. He glanced at Heather. "Didn't you say that you'd just seen your doctor? Is she still in the building?"

She nodded. "Dr. Sharon Moreno. She's on the top floor."

"Her doctor is in this building. Sharon Moreno. Top floor. Please notify her. We're going to need help here."

"Will do."

There were a couple of clicks, then silence. A second later, the maintenance guy was back. "She'll be down in five minutes to talk to you."

Jim turned to Heather. "They're getting your doctor. Can you scoot over this way so you can talk to her? The receiver won't reach to where you're sitting."

Heather pushed a strand of blond hair off her cheek and tucked it behind her right ear. "You talk to her. I don't want to move. Everything hurts." She breathed slowly and steadily, her eyes closed.

Again, she tensed in pain. She was so thin he would have sworn he could see her belly rippling with the force of her contraction. He ached to do something to help her. Instead, he could only sit there, waiting for the doctor.

She groaned softly and wrapped her arms around her belly. "It hurts," she breathed shakily. "I'm scared, Jim. I know you don't want to hear that, but I am."

"I understand." He reached down and took her hand in his. "It's okay to be scared. I'm right here with you. I'm not going anywhere."

Her mouth twitched. "You couldn't even if you wanted to."

"I know, but even if I could, I wouldn't leave."

"Really?" Her startled gaze met his. "You swear?"

He nodded. "You don't have to be alone through this. I give you my word."

"Thank you."

Just then, a woman's voice came on the line. "This is Dr. Moreno. Is that you, Heather?"

"No, Doctor. My name is Jim Dyer. I'm in the elevator with Heather. She's in labor."

"Can I talk to her?"

Jim looked at Heather and knew she wasn't moving on her own. "Yeah. Give me a second." He let the receiver dangle. "Heather, the doctor wants to talk to you. Let me help you shift closer so you can reach the receiver."

She was shaking her head in refusal even as she began to inch toward him. He knelt beside her and eased one arm under her legs and the other behind her back.

"Are you having a labor pain?" he asked.

"Not right now."

"On the count of three." He counted, then drew her against him and moved her next to the phone.

She took a couple of breaths before she picked up the receiver. "So much for waiting a few more days. I guess you were wrong, Dr. Moreno," she said with a touch of humor. "First time ever?"

There was a pause while she listened to her doctor.

"They're about three minutes apart," she said. "The pain is intense. It feels like—" She gasped and thrust the phone at Jim, then panted as her body twisted.

"She's tough," Jim said to the doctor as he held on to Heather's hand, "but this is hard for her."

"For both of you," the doctor said. "Do you have any medical training?"

He told her about his first-aid classes in the service.

"First babies are notoriously tardy," Dr. Moreno told him. "However, based on the fact that Heather's water has already broken and the duration and frequency of her labor pains, we'll have to assume she might not wait for the elevator to be fixed. I want to explain a few things to you in case you have to deliver the child. Have you ever seen a baby born before?''

"Not really," he muttered.

Jim felt as if someone had kicked him in the gut. Watching Heather in labor was one thing, but having her doctor say he might have to help her deliver her baby was another. He wanted to insist that Dr. Moreno call the words back, but he couldn't. He was all Heather had. It was up to him to get her through this.

She explained about the stages of labor and what was probably happening to Heather and the baby. She had him lower Heather onto her back and help her with her breathing. The contractions continued. He breathed as the doctor told him, setting a pace for Heather to follow as the pains got longer and came closer and closer together.

"It hurts," Heather moaned after a particularly long and intense set of contractions.

"I know. You can do this."

Jim mouthed the words because they were all he had. He kept holding her hand and breathing with her, all the while wondering why something as wonderful as childbirth had to be so damn hard on the mother.

The small room seemed to close in around him. He couldn't tell if it was getting hot or just his reaction to the stress. Even as he urged Heather to hang on, he kept listening for a sound or waiting for a gentle lurch that would tell him the elevator was back in working order.

"I want to push," Heather gasped.

"Don't!" Jim instructed as he squeezed her fingers with one hand and wiped the sweat from her face with the other. He had the receiver cradled between his shoulder and ear. ''She wants to push,'' he told the doctor.

''Tell her not to. You're going to have to check and see if the baby has crowned. If it has, you'll be able to see the top of the head. That means she's ready to deliver.''

Jim swallowed. He didn't want Heather to be ready to deliver. He also didn't want to have to look to find out. ''Be right back with you,'' he said, and let go of the phone.

''What is it?'' Heather asked.

The hem of her cotton dress rested on her thighs. Two hours ago, he hadn't even met this woman. He couldn't possibly do this. ''The doctor wants me to check on the baby. She thinks I might be able to see the head.''

Heather's big eyes got bigger. ''I can't believe I'm going to have my baby right here in an elevator!''

''Tell me about it.''

He braced himself for tears. Instead, much to his surprise, she smiled weakly. ''Talk about a great story when she's growing up.'' Then her humor faded. She looked at him, then down at herself. For the first time since her labor started, color stained her cheeks. ''I don't think I can get my panties off on my own.''

''Right.'' He cleared his throat. This would be easier for both of them if he pretended this was a completely normal situation, something that had to be done but wasn't the least bit personal. Without looking, he reached under the full skirt of her dress and peeled off her underpants. He folded them neatly and set them in the corner. ''Uh, I'm supposed to check on the baby,'' he said, not able to meet her gaze.

"I know. I'm sorry."

"You don't have to apologize."

"I feel like I do. You sure didn't ask for this."

Her voice was so small he couldn't help looking at her face. She bit her lower lip, then panted through another contraction. This time, he *could* see her stomach twisting and rippling as her body truly labored to bring forth life. Her face contorted in a grimace.

"Under normal conditions, you might have trouble explaining how you came to be with a strange, half-naked woman in an elevator," she said, gasping. "So you'll have a story to tell, too."

"I can't wait," he told her.

Another contraction ripped through her. She screamed out, then gripped his hand with a strength that nearly snapped a couple of bones.

"If this doesn't scare you into practicing safe sex, nothing will," she managed to say, her face covered in sweat. "Look, Jim, I'm in way too much pain to be embarrassed right now, so go ahead and look for the baby. I just want to make sure that my child is safe. Please?"

He nodded, then steeled himself against the inevitable. He peered around the side of her knee. "I can't see anything."

A sharp sound filled the elevator. He looked at Heather. Despite the pain and her gasping breath, she was laughing. "You kept your eyes closed. You're going to have to open them to see something."

He felt like a moron. "I don't think I can."

"Of course you can. Pretend I'm a giraffe and this is *National Geographic.*"

She didn't look like a giraffe, but he didn't intend

to let her down. He knelt between Heather's feet, then pushed back her dress and studied her body.

He straightened and grabbed the phone. "I think I see the top of the baby's head."

"Damn," Dr. Moreno muttered. "She's determined to deliver quickly. Wouldn't you know it? Okay, Jim. Tell Heather not to push even though she wants to. As the baby begins to appear, apply a very gentle pressure to keep the head from coming out too fast. Don't force anything, don't pull."

He repeated the instructions back to make sure he understood them, then did as the doctor had instructed. She took him step by step through the process. Heather resisted the urge to push, working hard to control her reaction to the intense contractions.

"I can't," she screamed. "Make it stop. Let me push."

"Don't do it!" Jim ordered. "Stay with me, Heather. We've come this far. Just trust me. You're fine. Relax and breathe. Breathe with me. I'm right here. I'll catch your baby, Heather. I'll be right here. Just a little bit more."

Ten minutes later, he set a tiny, red squalling baby on her mother's belly.

"It's a girl," he said, not quite able to believe he'd actually helped bring a child into the world.

Heather tried to raise her head enough to see, but she was too weak. "Is she okay?"

"Ten fingers and ten toes," he said as he stared at the messy, naked, incredible creature squirming and squawking with life. "And she's just as beautiful as her mother."

The doctor gave him a few final instructions and

said that she would be standing by when they finally got the elevator working. As Jim hung up the phone, Heather started to cry. For once, the sight of a woman's tears didn't bother him. He understood completely, and if he hadn't been so tired and excited at the same time, he might have shed one or two himself. This wasn't a moment either of them could have described to someone else. They'd done something extraordinary together and there weren't any words to explain it. So instead of speaking, he moved next to Heather and pulled her into his arms, shifting her so that she could gaze down at her baby. As she tightened her hold on her child, he tightened his hold on her.

"Thank you for not leaving me," she said as she cradled her infant. The baby girl quieted, safe in her mother's embrace.

He rested his chin on the top of her head. "Is this where I point out that I had nowhere else I could go?"

"You know what I mean. You weren't just in the room, you were helping. That means a lot to me." She sniffed. "I'm a mess and I can't believe I cried. I never cry."

"I think you'll be forgiven this one time. There was a lot going on."

"I know, but still…" She shook her head. "Look at this poor elevator car. It looks like we shot a scene from a horror film here. They'll have to replace the carpet."

"Quit worrying about stuff like that. You have a brand-new, beautiful baby."

"I know. Isn't she wonderful?"

She was. Jim didn't let himself think about kids too

much, but when he did, he admitted that the longing to have a few of his own was still there. "Everybody says birth is a miracle," he said, "but I didn't get what that meant until today."

"Me neither."

The baby in her arms opened her tiny eyes. He knew it wasn't possible, but he would have sworn that the child could see clear down to his empty soul. Suddenly, the elevator lurched slightly.

Heather stiffened. "Is that what I think it is?"

"I sure hope so."

Sure enough, a second later they heard the sound of the motor, and the car began gently moving down to the ground floor. The doors opened and two medics and Dr. Moreno stepped into the car. Jim started to stand up. Heather grabbed his arm.

"I know this is asking a lot," she said, "but would you mind coming with me to the hospital? I'm just..." She bit her lower lip.

"I know," he said as he rose to his feet. "I'd like to come with you. I want to make sure you and the little one are okay." He glanced down at his slacks and grinned. The khaki fabric was covered in blood. "Besides, the hospital is the only place I can think of where they'll let me in dressed like this."

By three o'clock that afternoon, Heather and her daughter had been examined and pronounced none the worse for their adventure.

"Next time, you might want to think about getting to the hospital a little earlier," a nurse whispered as she finished taking Heather's blood pressure.

Heather laughed. "I'll do my best."

"At least your husband was with you," the nurse continued as Jim entered the room. "I'm sure that was a big help."

"I couldn't have done it without him," Heather said honestly, figuring there was no point in explaining the fact that a complete stranger had come to her aid.

The nurse gave her a quick smile, then left. Jim moved close to the bed and looked down at her.

"I've only got a couple of minutes," he said. "I need to get home, shower and change, then head back to the office, but I wanted to make sure you were feeling all right."

"We're both fine. They checked her out—" she nodded at the infant she cradled in her arms "—and she's doing great. Strong heart, clear lungs, responsive. Dr. Moreno said it was a textbook delivery and she couldn't have done better herself."

"Yeah, like I believe that." Jim shoved his hands into his slacks pockets. "She stopped me in the hall and congratulated me. I didn't have the heart to tell her I'd been terrified the whole time."

"You didn't show it," Heather said.

"That was the point. If anyone had the right to be scared, it was you. I didn't want to add to your stress."

"Thank you for everything."

She'd already said the words a dozen times, but it still wasn't enough. She didn't know how she'd be able to thank this man for all he'd done for her. She stared up at him and was suddenly struck again by his good looks. He had the kind of body that belonged in an underwear ad. Shaggy dark hair hung to his shirt collar and fell across his forehead. Right now, though, he looked a little worse for wear. His clothes were wrinkled and stained, and he had the stunned expression of someone who had lived through a natural disaster or a plane crash.

They were both silent. Heather noticed Jim fidgeting slightly, shifting from foot to foot.

"Me, too," she murmured.

"You, too, what?"

She shrugged, then brushed her finger gently across the soft cheek of her newborn child. The child she'd fallen in love with the moment she'd seen her. "I'm confused. I don't know what to say or how to say it. We've just shared possibly the most intimate experience of my life. I can't say about yours." She smiled up at him. "For all I know, you do this sort of thing regularly."

"I promise this was my first time." He paused. "I'm glad I was there for you."

"Not as glad as I am. I want…" She felt her throat tightening. It was just the emotional aftermath of all that had happened. At least that's what she told herself. "I want to thank you."

"You have. About twenty-five times. You're welcome."

She shook her head. "No, I really want to thank you, but I can't think of the right words, and when I try, I get all weepy." She shuddered. "I never cry. Seriously, I break down in tears maybe once every four or five years. I cried on the elevator earlier today so that's it for me for a while. The thing is, I can't seem to get my self-control back."

"Hey, kid, you just gave birth. I think tears are

allowed. Although I'll admit I'm a normal guy and they're not my favorite thing to see on a pretty face like yours.''

She knew he meant the compliment in a friendly way. It didn't *mean* anything. After all, she knew she was pale and that her hair was a mess, not to mention she was wearing an incredibly unflattering hospital gown. But that didn't stop a very female flash of appreciation for his kind words.

"You're a good man, Jim Dyer," she said.

"Yeah, yeah, and you appreciate everything I did. But you did all the hard work. I only had to catch this pretty girl." He stroked her daughter's tiny hand. "I'm glad you're both fine. Really."

He wasn't going to let her say everything she was feeling. It was probably better for both of them because she wasn't sure what she was feeling. Still, she had to try. "I'm being serious."

"So am I." He leaned toward her. "Tell you what. If it will make you feel better, you can name her after me. Jimmy with an 'i' or something."

"What's your middle name?"

"Michael."

"That could work." She laughed. "I'll give it some thought."

"Don't you dare." His blue gaze settled on her child. "She's too perfect to be saddled with a name like that. Give her a beautiful name, like yours."

"I'll do my best."

"The two of you are going to be very happy," he said, then stopped speaking, but she read the questions in his eyes. Questions about her past and why she was raising this child alone. Heather thought about answering them but wasn't sure what to say. If Luke hadn't been such a jerk, she wouldn't be in this position. But he had been, and she was. She would make the best of it.

"I know what you're thinking," she told him. "I'm nervous, but I'm not scared. My mom was a single parent and I think she did a great job."

"You will, too," he said confidently. "You're tough and you're a fighter."

"You got all that from one elevator ride?"

"It was the ride of my life." He squeezed her shoulder. "I need to be going. I'll check on you later."

"You don't have to," she said automatically. Even as the words came out, she wanted to call them back. She *did* want Jim to look in on her before she went home. It didn't make any sense, but they'd shared something deeply personal and she wasn't ready to let that go yet.

"I want to," he assured her. "Besides, you might change your mind about the ex-boyfriend. The offer still stands. I'll beat him up for you."

It was a ridiculous thing for him to say and the sweetness of his misplaced gesture made her eyes burn with tears. Definitely hormones, she told herself even as she had to clear her throat before speaking.

"I appreciate the offer, but I'm still refusing it. I'll admit I've learned some valuable lessons in the past few months. I'm not a man hater, but I'm a little wary of the gender. I've been telling myself it was better to learn about Luke's character before my child was born and I've reached the point where I actually believe that. I'm better off without him. The baby and I are going to be fine.''

"I never doubted that for an instant.'' Jim bent down and kissed her forehead. "Get some rest. I'll see you this evening.'' He pulled a card from his pocket and dropped it on the table next to her bed. "That's my number. If you think of anything you need or you want me to bring, just call and let me know.''

"Thank you. Bye.''

She watched him walk away. For some reason, the spot where he'd kissed her forehead tingled a little. She told herself to ignore the sensation. Men like Jim were too good to be true. He was probably an angel or someone sent to her in her time of need and she would never see him again.

The image of Jim in wings made her chuckle. Then a dull pain shot through her belly, reminding her that she'd been struggling to give birth not so very long ago.

"You surprised everyone,'' she told her perfect little girl. "Here I thought I had plenty of time to get to my car and drive home. But you fooled us all. Does that make you happy?''

The tiny infant barely stirred.

"I love you so much. You and I are going to have a wonderful life together.''

Her daughter made a cooing sound in her sleep. Heather felt her heart fill with love and gratitude. Everything had turned out perfectly.

Chapter Three

That evening, Heather found herself watching the doorway to her room with a ridiculous impatience. Jim Dyer didn't owe her anything, least of all a visit. He had just been kind earlier when he'd said he would drop by and check on her. No doubt he'd had a chance to think about all they'd been through together and he'd decided that the situation had been too stressful and embarrassing and not one he wanted to relive.

Under the circumstances, she couldn't blame him. He'd been a Good Samaritan, but now he'd returned to his regular life. She and her daughter would be fine on their own. Besides, it's not as if he would have done anything but say hello, then leave.

But all the cheerful, determined, logical words in the world weren't making her feel any better. She wanted to pick up the business card he'd left her and call him. She wanted him to walk into her room and tell her...

At this point, her imagination failed her. What exactly did she want him to say? Nothing romantic. She'd given birth that afternoon, and even if she was in a position to pursue a relationship, which she wasn't, she'd sworn off men, at least for the next fifty years or so. Besides, Jim might be married or engaged or simply not interested. Not that she wanted him to be interested. She didn't. She wanted...

"Hormones," she muttered to herself. All the books on pregnancy warned that after she gave birth, her body would be awash with lots of hormones, most of which had the unfortunate side effect of making her emotions run wild. She drew in a deep breath to calm herself. She was a strong, capable woman with a beautiful new baby and a bright future. The fact that she was feeling a little out of sorts was completely normal. She would give herself a break. It was perfectly fine to *want* to see the man who had helped her through a difficult time, but it wasn't all right to *do* something about seeing him.

That plan of action—or inaction—decided, she turned her attention to the sleeping child in her arms. The nurse had told her it was acceptable to let her daughter sleep in the bassinet pulled up to the side of the bed, but Heather liked the feel of the slight weight of her baby pressed against her. When her arms got tired, she would put the child down, but for now, this was perfect.

Her eyes drifted closed and she might have slept. The next thing she heard was a faint knocking. She came to with a start and saw Jim standing just inside the door to her room.

"I didn't mean to wake you," he said. "I can come back later."

Her mouth went dry. It wasn't supposed to, of course. She told herself it must be the result of not having enough to drink or the air-conditioning in the large hospital. It certainly wasn't because of the man standing in front of her. A tall, handsome man dressed in a shirt and jeans, which should have looked ordinary but instead made her think that he was too good-looking to be real.

"I'm awake," she managed. Not exactly the brilliant conversational opening she'd been practicing earlier, but her nap had apparently cleared her brain of all coherent thought. She felt herself smiling. "Thanks for coming to see me."

"No problem," he said as he stepped into the room. "I'm visiting all my patients to see how they are. So how *are* you doing?"

"We're great." She nodded at her daughter. "She had her first meal, and according to the nurse, it went well." She grimaced, remembering the unexpected strength of the baby tugging on her breast. "Actually, it was easier for her than for me. Except for the excitement, she's mostly slept. I've had a bracing walk around my room and I ate dinner. All in all, a full and exciting day."

"You look great," he said, then swallowed as if he hadn't meant to blurt that out.

"Thanks." She touched her freshly washed hair. "They let me take a shower. I feel a lot better."

"These are for you." He set a large plant and an

even bigger stuffed giraffe on the small table by the window.

It took Heather a second to remember her advice in the elevator to pretend she was a giraffe about to give birth. The silly gesture touched her and she felt herself tearing.

Jim held up his hands and took a step back. "Wait a minute. You promised you cried once every four or five years. I figured I was safe."

She waved toward the chair next to her bed. "You are. It's all of my hormones out of whack, I guess. I'm completely not myself. But I will struggle to maintain control. Thank you for the gifts. They're incredibly thoughtful and you really didn't have to."

"I wanted to." He settled in the chair and grinned. "You should've seen the look the dry cleaner gave me when I dropped off my slacks. I told him what happened, but I don't think he believed me." He stared at her. "And to answer the question I know you're thinking, no, you may not pay for the dry cleaning."

"If I insist?" she asked.

"I'll ignore you."

She told herself his assumption that she would offer to pay was just a natural extension of their conversation, but she couldn't shake the odd feeling that he'd somehow read her mind.

He leaned back and rested one ankle on the opposite knee. The masculine pose reminded her that Jim was a stranger in her life. She didn't know anything about him, yet she felt oddly connected to him.

"This is very strange," she confessed. "I'm not

sure what we should talk about or what I'm supposed to say. I want to keep thanking you for everything—''

"Please don't," he said quickly. "I know you're glad I was with you and I'm glad I was there, too. End of story." He gave a slight shrug. "But I know what you mean about the situation being unusual. I've never walked up to a woman and said, 'Hi, I'm Jim Dyer. Let me help you give birth.'''

"You did a great job so I'm sure pregnant women will be lining up to have you there with them."

He shuddered. "Once was enough. If I ever get married and have kids, I want them to make their appearance in the hospital surrounded by plenty of doctors and nurses."

"Gee, that's exactly what I want for my next baby, too." She made sure her voice was calm and told herself the fact that he'd just told her he wasn't married didn't change anything. She wasn't looking for a man. Not even one who'd been so sweet to her.

Jim glanced around the room. There was a huge bouquet of balloons tied to the foot of her bed. "You've had visitors?" he asked.

Heather shook her head. "Those are from my mom. I talked to her a couple of hours ago. She feels terrible about not being with me right now. I keep telling her everything is fine, but she worries."

"Where is she?"

"Florida. Her husband, my stepfather, recently had heart surgery. He's doing great, but she's nervous about leaving him on his own. I keep telling her I understand. When I was growing up, she was always there for me, so I don't mind doing this on my own."

He frowned. "You don't have anyone to stay with you when you get out of here?"

"It's not a big deal."

Jim shifted, placing both feet flat on the floor and leaning toward her. "When do they release you?"

"Tomorrow."

He straightened. "That soon?"

"Yes. We're both healthy and I'm ready to go home." She wanted to get a start on spending time with her daughter, not to mention sleeping in her own bed.

He didn't look convinced. "You don't sound worried."

"I'm not."

"You're a lot tougher than you look, but then, I already knew that." He reached out and stroked her daughter's arm. "You've got one determined mother there. Looks like you come from hardy stock."

The baby opened her eyes and stared solemnly at Jim. "Do you want to hold her?" Heather asked impulsively.

Instantly, he pulled his hands back and shook his head. "That's okay. I'm sure she's more comfortable with you than with a stranger."

"She was born less than twelve hours ago. I think we're all still strangers to each other. Come on, it's easy."

He looked trapped as he rose to his feet and stood beside the bed. "I'm not going to be good at this," he grumbled.

"Yes, you are. Now look at how I have her in my arms. You have to be careful to hold her head, but otherwise, don't worry. Just cradle her gently and relax.''

She leaned forward a little. Jim bent toward her and took the baby, his arm brushing hers. He shifted the tiny bundle until she was secure in the crook of his left elbow. He looked big and awkward standing there, but the expression of sheer wonder on his face melted her heart.

"She's amazing," he said, his voice laced with awe. "So perfect." One big finger stroked the back of her tiny hand. "Hi there," he murmured. "Aren't you the pretty one?" He glanced at Heather. "She's staring at me with that worried expression all babies seem to have. Do you think they know they're a big responsibility and are thinking that their parents might not be up to the task?"

Heather laughed. "I have no idea what's on her mind."

He returned his attention to the infant. "You'll be just fine, sweet cheeks. You have a great mom. You're going to grow up to be smart and beautiful, but you better watch out for boys. They can be lots of trouble."

Heather's heart filled with pride and love for this child she'd brought into the world. For a second, she felt a flash of regret that she was in this alone. It would be wonderful to have a man sharing in her joy and love. Heather would do her best to be all things to her daughter, but there would be times when the little girl would miss having a father. Heather had from time to time, despite her mother's support and kindness.

But that wasn't in the cards for her. Luke didn't

want anything to do with this child and Heather no longer wanted him in her life. And if she was even half as good as her own mother was to her, her baby would grow up in a house filled with love.

As she watched Jim with her daughter, she tried to ignore the erratic thoughts racing through her head. She couldn't help noticing how appealing he was— the big, strong man holding the tiny baby. This was the stuff of greeting cards and television commercials. Oddly touching and romantic, which was crazy. More of those hormones, she told herself.

"I've named her," Heather said.

Jim looked up and grinned. "Really? What?"

"Diane Michelle. My mom's name is Diane and the Michelle part is for Michael."

He stared at her, his expression stunned. She could read his thoughts as easily as if he spoke them aloud. "You didn't have to do that," Jim said quickly. "I was teasing you about naming her after me."

"I know, but I wanted to do something meaningful to thank you. I wouldn't have been able to get through giving birth to her if you hadn't helped me. You did more than I could ever have hoped for. You made something that could have been scary and awful into the most wonderful experience of my life." She paused. "I picked Michelle because I couldn't come up with a female version of James that I liked as well."

He stared at her a long time. She looked into his impossibly handsome face and told herself that while he might look very silly with wings, this man was definitely an angel.

"Thank you," he said. "I'm speechless, which, my

friends will tell you, is a rarity.'' He glanced down at the baby. ''Hello, Diane Michelle. Welcome to this world. Don't you ever forget how special you are.'' He handed the baby back to Heather and sat back down. ''She's so small. I can't believe they're letting you take her home tomorrow.''

''She's nearly seven pounds,'' Heather informed him. ''That's plenty big.''

Jim didn't look convinced. ''How are you getting home?''

Heather knew exactly what he was asking, but she decided to pretend ignorance. ''By car.''

''You have a friend to take you?''

She didn't have to see his face to know he was worrying about her. If she told him the truth—that she planned to call a cab—he would be offended. While it would be nice to be fussed over for a while, it was better for her to begin as she meant to continue, and that meant being responsible for herself.

''I have made arrangements, but it's very sweet of you to worry.'' She flashed him her best smile, hoping it would be enough to distract him.

It wasn't.

His gaze narrowed. ''What are you hiding?''

''Nothing. I have a ride. I'm fine.'' She nodded at Diane. ''We're fine.''

''Right. I'll be here at eleven in the morning.''

''Jim, no. That's silly.''

''Then give me the name of your friend.'' When she hesitated, he muttered something under his breath, something she was reasonably confident was unfit for a child's ears. ''You were going to take a cab, weren't you?''

She'd never been very good at lying. Even now, she could feel color creeping into her face. "I didn't want to impose. I'm not your responsibility. In fact, we don't know each other at all."

He stiffened in the chair, then straightened. "You're right. I'm sorry, I didn't mean to intrude. I can see why you would be concerned. Under the circumstances—"

"Stop," she interrupted. "Please." She could read the truth in his withdrawn expression. "I did not mean to imply that I'm worried you're an ax murderer or that you have some evil designs. When I said we were strangers, I meant I didn't have the right to inconvenience you. If you were an old friend or family, then I would impose at will. I swear, that's all I was trying to say. Just that I don't want you to feel obligated."

"I don't feel that way. I only want to help."

He had an honest face. Based on what she'd learned about him during their short acquaintance, she knew he was a good man. She'd met enough of the other kind to be able to recognize the difference. Part of her was wary, though, not believing he could really be all that he seemed, but as she had no intention of getting involved with Jim Dyer, what could it possibly hurt to accept his offer?

She drew in a deep breath. "To be honest, I hated the idea of taking a cab home. So if it wouldn't be too much of an imposition, I would appreciate a ride. Eleven is perfect. We'll be ready."

Jim smiled then, a dazzling smile that set up a chain reaction all the way down to the pit of her stomach. He rose to his feet.

"I should let you two get your rest. It's been a challenging day. I'll see you tomorrow morning."

"Okay. Thanks for coming by."

"My pleasure."

She had the oddest feeling that he was about to bend over and kiss her cheek, but all he did was wave and walk out of the room. As she settled back on the bed, Heather couldn't figure out why she suddenly felt disappointed and very much alone.

Jim pulled up in front of the hospital at ten minutes before eleven the next morning. He was pleased that Heather had decided to let him take them home. He didn't want to think about her having to carry anything heavier than the balloons. This way, he could take care of any lifting or moving of Diane and her car seat.

Over the next few days he planned to make sure Heather didn't have anything to worry about. He'd made that decision the previous evening. When he got home, he hadn't been able to sleep. All through the night he'd found himself thinking about Heather and what they'd shared. He'd never imagined what it would be like to help a woman give birth. Even though he'd always had the vague idea that one day he would have children, it wasn't something he'd allowed himself to dwell on. Too many unhappy memories, he thought. But if the situation ever came up, he now had some experience.

He headed to the maternity wing and found Heather up and dressed, sitting in the chair beside her bed, holding Diane. The tiny infant was asleep, and the sight of her cradled in her mother's arms hit him like a sucker punch to the belly. All his air rushed out and he was left gasping for breath.

It should have been like this for him. The unwelcome thought came unbidden. He'd pushed the past so far back in his mind that he hadn't thought it could possibly find its way to the light. But it had. It should have been like this for him, he thought again. But Carrie had never given him the chance.

At that moment, Heather glanced up and saw him. "Hi," she said with a smile. "Right on time, but then I guess she's the only one around here who's chronically early," she added, nodding toward her daughter.

Heather wore a loose-fitting dress and sandals. There was a lot less tummy than before, although her midsection was still a little out of proportion compared with her thin arms and legs. Her hair had been pulled back into a ponytail and her face was bare of makeup. She looked young and excited, as if she was beginning the most wonderful adventure.

"Morning," he said. "I see you're all packed."

Several shopping bags stood by the door, as did an infant car seat. "My apartment manager stopped by my place on her way to work and got me a few things," she told him. "Including the car seat. Although I have to warn you, I'm not exactly sure how to strap it in. The directions are in the box."

"I'm sure I can figure it out." He grabbed the infant seat in one hand and scooped up the shopping bags in the other. "I'll head out to the car, then come back and get you."

"The nurse said they had to wheel me out, so we'll meet you out front."

He nodded and left. After stowing the bags in the trunk, he removed the car seat from its box and glanced at the directions. They seemed simple enough to him, and fifteen minutes later, the seat was firmly secured in the back. He straightened and turned to see Heather and Diane being wheeled out of the main entrance to the hospital.

As they approached, she caught sight of the car seat in place. "You've got the thing installed already," she said, her voice accusing.

"Of course."

"It must be a guy thing. I really hate that. It would've taken me an hour to figure it out."

He stepped back to let her put Diane into the carrier and strap her in. "The point is, you would have figured it out eventually. It doesn't matter how long it takes."

"Easy for you to say, Mr. I-Can-Fix-It-In-Seconds."

He grinned. "Some of us have it, and some of us don't."

"Very funny." Heather closed the rear door and turned to thank the nurse's aid. Then she slowly lowered herself into the passenger seat.

"Still sore?" he asked.

"Yeah. In places I didn't know could hurt this much. But the nurses all tell me it will get better quickly."

He made sure she was settled before he circled around to the driver's side. There was something intimate about picking up a woman and her newborn from the hospital and taking them home. Something that screamed "family." The sensation didn't bother him. If anything, he was enjoying his chance to pretend that this was all his. He would take care of Heather for a while, then return to his solitary life. It was what he'd always done.

"Nice car," Heather said as he started the engine. "It's a BMW, right?"

"Yes, a 540, their midsize sedan. I also have a truck, which I drive most of the time, but I figured you and Diane would be more comfortable in this car, not to mention its having a trunk."

Her big green eyes widened slightly. "A truck *and* a BMW. The helicopter business must pay well. I didn't realize my baby was being delivered by a tycoon."

"Tycoon is a bit of a stretch, but the business does do well. Executives and rock stars like to travel by helicopter and that don't come cheap." He rested his hands on the steering wheel. "Where to?"

She named two cross streets in the southwest part of the valley and he headed that way. Traffic was relatively light. Heather leaned back in her seat and sighed. "This is nice. I could doze off right here."

"Did you get any sleep?"

"Not much. Some of it was discomfort, but mostly I think I was too excited. What with being a new mom and all. I figure I'll be back to work in about two weeks."

"What? You can't be serious. That's too soon."

She looked at him. "Not the factory. I have a three-month maternity leave from them, and if everything goes as planned, I'm not returning for several months after that, or even at all. I meant my bookkeeping business. There's an accountant who sends work my way, and I've found a few clients on my own. The practice is small, but it's growing. I work out of my home, so it's just a matter of shuffling to the computer and working on the books. I'm hoping to pick up a couple more clients, then I'll only need to get a part-time job to supplement my income. I would prefer to stay home as much as possible with Diane.''

''You have it all worked out.''

''I hope so. I've known I was going to be a single parent almost from the beginning of my pregnancy, so I've been able to make plans.''

Heather was tough and together and had many other qualities he admired. At the next red light, he took a minute to study her profile. She had a straight nose and full lips. Pale skin made her eyes look big and dark green. She was blond and pretty. It would be very easy for men to be attracted to her. But what he liked most wasn't her looks despite the fact that he found her appealing. Instead, he admired her character and her strength of will.

He caught the scent of something familiar. It took him a second to figure out it was baby powder and the sweet fragrance of the infant sleeping behind them. The situation was strange, he admitted.

''Do you realize that only twenty-four hours ago, you had just stepped into the elevator?'' he said.

She glanced at the clock on the dashboard. ''I know. So much has happened.'' She pointed to the corner. ''Turn right here. Then it's the second street on your left.''

The neighborhood was older, well kept, but it hadn't been revitalized. Large trees raised some of the curbs and the long branches nearly touched over the center of the street.

"It's 1434," she said, directing him to a freshly painted duplex. The cream stucco was accented by gray trim. "I have the back unit. It has a yard, which is going to be great for Diane."

He pulled into the driveway.

"Park in front of the garage door on the right," she said. "That's mine. The entrance is around to the side."

It took two trips to get Heather, Diane and their belongings into the small rear apartment. The second time he crossed the threshold, he found Heather pulling open drapes to let in the bright May sunshine and warm southern California air.

"One of the reasons I rented this place was the garden," she said.

Jim crossed the room to stand beside her. The backyard was surprisingly large, with several trees and a row of rosebushes along a painted white fence. There were squares of freshly sprouted vegetables to the right, and on the left, a patch of brightly colored flowers.

"You've put a lot of work into it," he said.

"It's how I relax. There's nothing like digging in the dirt to make me forget my troubles." She waved one hand to indicate the living room. "I know it's not much, but it's mine."

The room was large with a tweed sectional sofa in warm earth tones while colorful rugs were scattered across a worn hardwood floor. There were plants in baskets, several small tables with books and magazines, and a television that looked at least a half-dozen years old. Behind him was the eating area, with a light oak round table and four chairs. The whole place was clean and neat, with a welcoming, homey feeling. Heather obviously didn't have a lot of money to spend, but she'd made the most of what she had.

"I like it," he said.

"Want to see Diane's room?" she asked shyly.

"Sure."

He followed her down a short hallway. On the left, through an open doorway, he caught sight of a bed covered with a white lacy spread. There were piles of pillows and lace curtains at the windows. Without wanting to, he could picture Heather stretched out on that bed, her arms open, waiting for him....

He shook off the thoughts, telling himself they were worse than inappropriate. The woman had given birth the day before. She didn't know him from a rock and she trusted him to be a decent person. He wasn't about to let her down. So what if he thought she was attractive and he liked her? His personal feelings had no bearing on the situation. He owed her respect and friendship, not lust and desire.

"She's in here," Heather said as she entered the bedroom on the right.

This room had clearly been intended as the master. It was big and had large windows that overlooked a side garden filled with flowering vines and roses. To the left, against the far wall, was a computer desk, two tall bookcases and three filing cabinets. The walls were cream and undecorated. But to the right, the room was a baby's idea of paradise. Yellow walls had been edged with a bunny rabbit border. Bright prints hung on the walls and there were soft fabric balloons floating down from the ceiling.

Heather stood next to a maple bassinet and gazed down at her daughter. "When I found out I was pregnant, I switched bedrooms," she said. "This way, I can spend the day with Diane and still be able to work. The computer is quiet enough to let her sleep, as is my laser printer." She touched the side of the bassinet. "One of my friends from the factory loaned me this for the first couple of months."

Jim glanced around and saw a white changing table. There was a partially assembled matching dresser and a narrow box containing a crib pushed up against a wall.

She followed his gaze. "I might be slow, but I'll get it all done."

"I don't doubt your ability," he said as he walked over to the dresser. It looked simple enough. "I could put these two pieces together—" he jerked his thumb toward the crib box "—in about two hours. I don't have the right tools with me, but I can bring them by later."

Heather shook her head. "You've done enough, Jim."

He went to stand next to her. "You've got to be tired and sore, not to mention feeling the weight of your new responsibility."

He glanced down at the sleeping baby. Her hair was a little darker than her mother's, but he could see the resemblance in the shape of her mouth and ears. No doubt as Diane got older, their relationship would be more obvious.

"But—"

He held up his hand to stop her. "Tell you what. I'm heading over to my office for a few hours. I'll call you around three. At that time you can give me a shopping list. Since you didn't plan to have your baby yesterday, I doubt you've got supplies in. Right?"

She stared at him. "Who are you? Why are you doing all this?"

"Because I want to," he answered lightly, dancing around the truth. He helped because it gave him the illusion of belonging and doing the right thing. Because these simple acts held the demons at bay. "Between now and then, make up a grocery list and I'll stop on my way over. If you're up to company, I'll put together the dresser and the crib. If you're worried about trusting me, I have references."

Diane stirred. Heather dropped her gaze to her child, then returned it to him. "Do you make a habit of rescuing people?"

"It's my hobby."

"I want to ask why, but I have a funny feeling you wouldn't tell me."

He didn't respond. They both knew she was right.

She tucked a loose strand of hair behind her ear and bit her lower lip. "I'm very tough and capable. I don't actually *need* you to help me."

"Agreed. But wouldn't it be nice to be able to let someone else take on some of the responsibility, even just for a couple of hours?"

She had long, pale lashes and a couple of freckles dotting her nose. Her full mouth turned up at the corners. "I would like to curl up and take a nap."

"So go for it. Write down your phone number, and

I'll call about three. Oh, and I need to move the car seat into your car. Which is probably still parked at your doctor's office. We'll talk about that later, too.''

"You're right…about all of it.'' She smiled. "I know it's probably getting boring to hear, but thank you. Again.''

"My pleasure,'' he said lightly, and he meant it. Not just because Heather appealed to him, but because helping her allowed him to pretend, if only for a while, that everything was fine.

Chapter Four

Heather opened the front door of her apartment and stared at Jim as he stood on the porch, a shopping bag in each hand. She didn't know whether to laugh or scream. "You're making me crazy," she said as she pushed open the screen door to let him in.

"You love all the attention," he said easily as he strolled into her kitchen and began putting away groceries. As if he was completely comfortable. As if he knew where everything went. Which he was and he did. The man had been visiting her twice a day for a week. Why wouldn't he be at home in her house?

"You can't keep buying me things," she said.

"Wanna bet?" He winked. "Besides, this isn't all for you."

"What have you bought her now?"

He tried to look innocent and instead only looked

sinfully handsome. Really, it was incredibly unfair. She wasn't getting a whole lot of sleep, so there were unattractive circles under her eyes. She had breasts for the first time in her life, which was nice except they hurt a lot and leaked, not to mention the fact that her clothes didn't fit right yet and she swam in her maternity stuff. Jim, on the other hand, was gorgeous. He frequently wore casual business dress or jeans, but he always looked put together, healthy and beautiful, if a man could be such a thing.

"Is she awake?" he asked instead of answering her question, then breezed past her and headed for Diane's room. Heather followed. "You're awake," he murmured to the baby in the bassinet. "Aren't you the clever girl, knowing that your uncle Jim was coming to see you?" He glanced at Heather. "May I pick her up?"

She nodded. Jim reached down and lifted Diane into his arms, then cooed at the infant.

"Did I tell you how pretty you are? That nightshirt Mommy chose is very flattering on you. It makes your eyes look even more blue. You're going to be a heart-breaker when you grow up. And smart, too. I can tell."

The litany went on. By now, Heather was used to Jim's ongoing conversations with her daughter. As far as he was concerned, little Diane was the most beautiful, brilliant, incredible child ever born. Lord knows what he would say if he had a kid of his own.

As Jim rocked and tickled and generally fussed over Diane, Heather tried to figure out who this man was. He had to have flaws, although to date she hadn't found any. He showed up with the regularity of a paid nurse, brought her groceries, stamps and any number of things she needed. He filled her car with gas so she could drive several hundred miles if circumstances called for it. He'd put together the dresser and the crib, had brought more toys than any three children could ever play with. He was funny and kind, fun to be with and the perfect gentleman. According to the brief rundown he'd given her on his life, he was single, had never been married and wasn't seriously involved with anyone. So why was he hanging out with an infant and her still-hormonal mother?

Heather didn't think of herself as a cynical person, but she'd seen a bit of the world. Men like Jim didn't exist. Therefore, there had to be something very, very wrong with him. If only she could figure out what it was....

Jim led the way back into the kitchen where he lifted a small pink bakery box out of a bag and set it on the table. He flashed Heather a grin. "You're welcome to join us if you'd like."

"Gee, thanks. If you don't think I'll be in the way."

He glanced down at the baby in his arms. "Do you think Mom will be in the way? I don't. I think she'll be a lot of fun at the party and I happen to know she's your favorite person in the whole world. So what do you say?" He paused as if Diane was answering, then nodded solemnly. "Diane says she's thrilled you're going to join us."

Despite her confusion and the unanswered questions she had about Jim, Heather had to laugh. "I'm honored." She took a seat across from him at the round table.

Jim pushed the bakery box toward her. "My hands are full right now. Why don't you open it?"

She lifted the lid and stared down at the little cake. Pink letters danced across chocolate frosting. It took her a minute to figure out that the letters weren't moving at all, but that they seemed to be because of the tears in her eyes. "Happy One Week B-day, Diane," read the script. Heather blinked rapidly so that Jim wouldn't see that her hormones were still acting up, then she removed the cake from the box and smiled at him.

"This is a very sweet gesture."

He beamed. "They couldn't spell out 'birthday' because there wasn't enough room, but I didn't think Diane would mind." He'd settled the baby so that her rump rested on the inside of his forearm and her head nestled by his shoulder. "Do you mind, sweet cheeks? It's chocolate, which I know is your favorite. Or it will be when you figure out what chocolate is. It's a girl thing. Women love chocolate. Guys do not understand this relationship, although we respect it." He kissed the top of her head. "You can't eat any today, but I wanted you to know I remembered your one week birthday. I thought for your one month celebration we'd have pony rides." He looked at Heather. "What do you think?"

"I think you're a very strange man." She got up and collected forks, a knife and two plates. "Do you want ice cream with your cake?"

"Sure." He shifted in his chair. "Uh-oh, this little one is fading fast."

Heather looked over and saw that her daughter had

closed her eyes and sagged against Jim. "Want me to take her to her room?"

"No," he told her as he rose to his feet. "I can do it."

With that, he disappeared into the rear of the house. Heather stared after him. When Diane had first been born, Jim had been afraid to hold her. He'd looked so awkward standing there in her hospital room. But a mere week later, he was an expert who even changed the occasional diaper. Just like a regular dad.

She paused in the act of slicing the cake. Jim Dyer wasn't Diane's father. He wasn't her anything. Luke was the biological parent, although since signing away his rights, he'd never gotten in touch with Heather. She wondered how he'd cut her out of his life so easily. Apparently, the relationship had been a game to him. Something he played at while he decided if he wanted to get back together with his wife.

"You're looking serious about something," Jim said from the kitchen doorway.

"Just lost in thought." She scooped ice cream onto both plates and set them on the table. "Thanks for this," she said as she pushed his dessert toward him. "You're right about women and chocolate."

"It's a scary thing," he teased. "I try not to think about it." He settled into the seat across from hers. "If it makes you feel any better, the lady at the bakery thought I was strange about the cake, too."

"I'll bet," Heather said, realizing the lady at the bakery would have assumed that Jim was a doting father.

Which brought her back to the question that had plagued her for an entire week. Why was he still here?

She poured them both tall glasses of milk, then sat at the table. "We have to talk," she said.

Jim paused in the act of raising a cake-and-ice-cream-laden fork to his mouth. He lowered his arm and pushed the plate away. "Sure. What do you want to talk about?"

If only he wasn't so good-looking, she thought uncomfortably as she took in the dark blue eyes and slightly too long hair that fell across his forehead. And that stupid dimple. How was she supposed to resist a man with a dimple? Especially a man who went out of his way to make her laugh and feel safe? Her mother would have told her to stop looking a gift horse in the mouth.

Ignoring what was probably very sound advice, Heather plunged ahead. "I want you to know that I appreciate everything you've done. The gifts, putting together the furniture. I think I could have finished the dresser, but that crib looked really tough. Most of all, I appreciate the visits and the conversation. I hadn't realized quite how trapped I would feel with a newborn. You've kept me from getting lonely and going stir-crazy." She paused, not sure how to continue.

"By your serious tone, I suspect you have more to say," Jim prompted gently.

She nodded. "This is very strange. Not you, but having you around. We don't know each other. Who are you and why are you in my life?"

He flashed her a quick smile. "This probably isn't a good time for my alien-abduction story, right?"

"It would explain certain things, but not in a way designed to make me feel comfortable."

He leaned forward as if to touch her hand, then stopped himself. Heather suffered through a brief flash of disappointment because she secretly, or maybe not so secretly, wouldn't have minded if he'd offered a little physical contact.

"When you ask who I am, I'm not sure how to answer," he said slowly. "I can give you my life history if that's what you're looking for. As for the reason why I'm in your life—well, that one's easier. I admire you, Heather, and I would like us to be friends. You're in a tough place at the moment. You're doing the right thing with your daughter, and I've learned that doing the right thing usually means taking a very difficult path. You don't have any family here, you don't have the father of your child to help. You have friends, but they have other commitments and can't always be around when you need them. I'm interested in filling in the gaps, nothing more."

He looked so incredibly earnest she wanted to believe him. Did he really admire her? She didn't think she'd ever done anything especially admirable in her life. In fact, she'd made a lot of silly choices. But she did try to do the right thing, especially now, with Diane depending on her.

"Why do you want us to be friends?" she asked.

He laughed. "What a question. I can't decide if you doubt yourself or me."

This time, he did lean forward and touch the back of her hand with his fingers. A startling heat flowed through her skin and up her arm. She did her best to ignore it.

"I like you," he said. "Why wouldn't I? You're

bright and funny, and we've shared the most amazing and embarrassing moment it's possible for two people to share, and we came out okay. I respect you. I think you like me. You know I can be counted on in a crunch. Many relationships have started with less and survived. But if this makes you too uncomfortable, I'll leave right now and you'll never hear from me again.''

His last statement made her stiffen. ''No, I don't want you to go,'' she told him, then wondered if she sounded too desperate or eager.

Why did relationships always get so complicated? Truth was, she liked having Jim around, but she didn't want anything more complicated than what they had.

''I can handle friendship,'' she said, allowing herself to briefly get lost in his gaze. ''But nothing more.'' Heat flared on her cheeks, and she forced herself to continue. ''Ever since things fell apart with Diane's father, I've sworn off men. I'm not looking for a relationship.''

Jim gave her fingers a quick squeeze, then released her with a dismissive gesture. ''You'll stay single for a while, but don't expect it to last. You're young and beautiful, and some guy is certain to come along and sweep you off your feet before you know what hit you. But if what you're trying to say is you wouldn't be comfortable taking our relationship to something more than friendship, that's fine with me.''

She couldn't get past the ''beautiful'' part to deal with the rest of his statement. Did he really think she was beautiful? She still had a puffy stomach and was too pale and too skinny everywhere else. Her hair needed cutting and she wasn't getting enough sleep or wearing enough makeup. Even so, his words sent a thrill of pleasure through her.

"I'm serious," she said, trying to keep her tone stern. "I'm not looking for love."

"Me neither. But I would like to be friends with both you and your daughter. She's stolen my heart."

"Mine, too," Heather admitted.

"Any other questions?" Jim asked.

She had dozens. Like why wasn't he off dating the supermodel of his choice? She sighed. Maybe her mother had been right. Maybe she should just accept this gift horse and be grateful he'd shown up in her life.

"No questions," she said. "I, too, would very much like us to be friends."

He picked up his fork and stabbed a big bite of cake and ice cream. "We already are."

Three weeks later, Heather dumped the basket of dry, clean laundry onto the sofa. Jim reached for the top item—a tiny undershirt. He smoothed it out and set it on the coffee table before grabbing another miniature garment.

Heather tried not to notice how careful he was with the scraps of clothing that weren't much bigger than his hand. She tried not to notice the lean lines of his body or the way he sprawled so comfortably on her sofa, as if he'd always belonged there.

"I've had two more phone calls from businesses wanting me to give bids on their bookkeeping services," she said as she folded a T-shirt of her own.

"That's nice." Jim didn't even look at her.

"I know what you're doing," she told him. "I've only known you for a month, but I'm completely on to you."

His expression was innocence itself. "I have no idea what you're talking about."

"Yes, you do, and I want you to stop it."

"Why? I know business owners who are interested in someone to take over their books. I also happen to know a bookkeeper who does great work. I'll admit I've made a couple of calls and given them your name, but what happens after that is up to them and you."

He made it sound so darn logical that she didn't know whether or not to smack him or thank him. "How do you know I'm good at what I do? Maybe I'm a lousy bookkeeper."

"Are you?"

"No, but you don't know that."

"Yeah, actually I do, Heather. You're just that kind of person. You're thorough and loyal. Did I mention dedicated? You're going to do a great job for them and probably for less than they're paying now. I haven't imposed on them or their relationship with me. If anything, I've done them a favor."

He was wearing jeans and a long-sleeved chambray shirt, rolled up to the elbows. His boots were scuffed but had obviously been expensive. She suspected the complicated-looking watch on his wrist had cost more than she'd made in the past quarter. He had a thriving business and who knows what kind of life, but he showed up nearly every day, called to check on her twice a day and couldn't seem to do enough for her.

"Why do you have to be so damned perfect?" she muttered.

Jim stared at her. "Heather Fitzpatrick, are you swearing? I'm shocked. And in front of your child, too."

"If you're shocked, then I'm secretly a mountain goat and I'm not swearing in front of my child. Diane is asleep in the other room, thank you very much."

He grinned, then picked up another tiny shirt. "Is she sleeping better?"

"Much. Several hours at a time. I'm longing for the first time she sleeps through the night."

"Still tired?"

"I think I'll be tired for about a year, but it's getting easier. I'm resting better and probably getting used to this constant state of exhaustion."

He asked about a new client, one he'd recommended. She began by explaining the mess the books were in, and before she realized what had happened, the laundry was folded and they were talking about dinner.

"How do you do that?" she asked as she leaned her head against the sofa back.

"Do what?"

"One minute we were talking about why you shouldn't be giving me clients and the next you've got me going on about my life. You always do that. When I try to talk about you, you change the subject by asking about me or the baby. Why don't you like to talk about yourself?"

He didn't even have the good grace to look annoyed that she'd caught him. Instead, he grinned. "I don't like to talk about myself because I already know everything that's happening in my life. It's more interesting to talk about you.'' He angled toward her on the sofa. ''What do you want to know, Heather?''

What she wanted was for her stomach to stop tingling every time he said her name. But instead of mentioning that, she asked, ''How did you come to own a helicopter charter company? Was it in the family?''

He shook his head. ''My dad was in construction. At least that's what he did when he walked out on me and my mom. I went to college and got my degree in engineering, then I went into the navy. I thought I wanted to fly jets until I went up in a helicopter with a buddy of mine. I knew then that I wasn't a flyboy at heart. I wanted more than flashy aircraft carrier takeoffs and landings in my career.''

''I'm sure fighter pilots really appreciate your assessment of their careers,'' she teased.

''They do.'' His smile faded. ''Actually, they work damn hard to get to fly those multimillion-dollar planes, and I respect that. But it wasn't for me. I learned to fly helicopters, and when my tour was up, I looked for a job that would let me fly them for a living.''

''You found one where you are now?'' she asked.

''Yeah. At first I was a charter pilot, then I started learning more about the business end of things. Mac—Philip J. Mackenzie—was the owner at the time. He'd grown the business up from nothing until he had a pretty steady clientele. I had some ideas about expanding and we agreed to go ahead with them. I put in my savings, he took me on as a partner, then when he retired, I bought him out.

"I still owe him three years of payments, then I'll own the company free and clear, though the way business is growing, I could cash him out tomorrow. I mentioned that to him recently and he told me to invest my money in new equipment. That he was happy to get his amount monthly. He said it kept him from playing the horses too much."

Heather shifted on the sofa. Her breasts were getting heavy. She glanced at the clock and figured Diane would be waking up hungry in the next half hour or so. "He sounds like a great guy."

"Mac's the best. I learned a lot from him. I wanted to move into renting and leasing helicopters as well as the charter service. Mac made me go slow and that paid off in the end. We never got too buried in debt."

There was a reverent and loving tone to his voice. Heather recognized it easily. Mac was more than a business partner to Jim—he'd been like a second father. She thought about Jim's brief comment that *his* father had walked out on him and his mother. He'd brushed over that fact as if it had no value or was of no interest.

But his father leaving had to have been hard on him. A boy needed his father. Was that the reason Jim was in her life? To give Diane what he had missed?

She realized that while Jim had talked a lot about his business, he hadn't told her anything personal. In fact, he rarely talked about himself. She knew only the barest details. What about the man inside? About what he felt and thought and dreamed?

She did know that he adored her daughter and seemed to like her. She also knew that he could make

her heart beat a little faster every time he walked into
a room. But little else. He always brought the conversation back to her and Diane.

She reminded herself that they were friends and
that he didn't owe her anything. Maybe he needed
more time to get comfortable. Maybe—

"Heather, I have something I want to talk to you
about."

He sounded so serious that her stomach knotted
into a ball. A thousand thoughts raced through her
brain. He'd gotten tired of visiting her. He'd figured
out that having him around was the closest thing
she'd had to a hot flash her entire life and he didn't
appreciate her staring at his well-formed, incredibly
tempting rear end. He thought she was raising her
daughter all wrong and he—

"Stop it," he commanded. "I don't know what
you're thinking, but forget it. Nothing I'm going to
say is worth that panicked expression in your eyes."

"I'm not panicked," she lied as she came face-to-
face with the uncomfortable realization that during
the past month Jim had become an important part of
her life. He was her most steady visitor and she de-
pended on him. If Jim were suddenly gone, she would
miss him terribly—perhaps even more than she'd ever
missed Luke.

"I've been talking to my accountant about using
your bookkeeping service," he began. "However, because of the way the books are set up and the computer program I use, there's no way for you to do
them at home. They have to be done at the office."

She stared at him. His books? This was about his
books? Disappointment flared through her. Then she

told herself to snap out of it. First she'd been terrified he was about to say he didn't want to be friends anymore. Now she was disappointed that he wanted to talk business? Obviously, she was still wrestling with some heavy-duty hormones from her pregnancy. She had to get a grip.

"So what I'd like to do," he continued, "is offer you a part-time job working for my company. I'll have my accountant show you the work and you pick your own hours." He leaned toward her. "I'm not asking just because we're friends. I'm asking because I know you'll do a good job for me. I meant what I said about picking your own hours. Whatever works best with your schedule and Diane's."

She was stunned. "I don't know what to say." He was offering her a job? With Jim, she frequently found herself in the position of not knowing whether to slap him or hug him, and here she was again.

"You can bring her in with you," he said before she could decide on a course of action. "There's a small storeroom off the main office that would make a perfect temporary nursery. Flo, the woman who manages the office, loves kids. She would be thrilled to have Diane around."

"I'll bet," Heather muttered. She was too confused to be having this conversation. Things were moving too fast. Although, knowing Jim, this conversation wasn't completely unexpected. "You're still trying to rescue me," she said. "I don't need rescuing. I'm perfectly capable—"

"Of taking care of yourself," Jim finished for her. "I know. All I'm saying is I need someone in my office. You need a part-time job. I don't care when you work and you need flexible hours. Besides, I'll be able to see my best girl more often.''

For a split second, she thought he meant her. Then reality returned to her brain and she knew he was talking about Diane. I will not be jealous of my own child, she told herself firmly.

''So what's the problem?'' Jim asked.

You are, she thought to herself, but couldn't say that aloud. He wouldn't understand. She knew that Jim was not for her. Even if he was, she wasn't interested in anything like that. So why was she tempted to accept his offer? It was crazy. She didn't want another man in her life, in any form. Their friendship was already straining the promise she'd made to herself not to get involved. She knew all the risks and pitfalls of a relationship with a man. She'd lived through every possible variation on that theme, with the possible exception of accidentally dating a man who was gay.

Except Jim wasn't talking about dating. He was talking about work. Was that safe? Could she stay friends with him and not get hurt? Was working for him crossing the line in some way?

She drew in a deep breath. The problem was that she was getting more and more involved. She needed him too much. This was the perfect time to tell him that their friendship was becoming too intense and that she wasn't comfortable. Working for him would only make things more difficult and complicated. She had to tell him no.

Chapter Five

"I never meant to agree to this," Heather said as she bent over her daughter's car seat and unbuckled the seat belt. "I said no, didn't I? I distinctly remember saying no."

But when she pulled out the car seat and straightened, she found herself staring at a large sign that read Valley Helicopter Services. If she hadn't taken the job that Jim offered her, what on earth was she doing here at his office?

Heather secured her purse more firmly over her shoulder, then closed and locked the car door before heading toward the main entrance to the building. There had to be a logical explanation, she told herself. A reason that she'd changed her mind. Unfortunately, she knew exactly what that reason was—Jim had made the part-time job impossible to turn down. Not only had he offered her a generous salary, the ability to set her own hours and the chance to work on an accounting program she'd wanted to learn for a long time, but he'd said she could bring Diane into the office with her. Which meant that she wouldn't have to pay for child care or worry about being apart from her infant.

Between this job and the other work Jim had sent her way, she was closer than ever to reaching her goal of a full-time home business. She didn't know that angels took the form of handsome six-foot-three-inch men, but she wasn't about to start complaining now. She'd had her chance to refuse and she hadn't, so for better or worse, she was about to become a part of Jim Dyer's world. Oddly enough, she found the thought more comforting than upsetting.

She paused in front of the glass double doors and drew in a deep breath for courage. She didn't doubt that she could do a good job for Jim. Working with numbers had always been easy for her and a real plea-sure. She was more concerned about how she would fit in with the rest of the employees. She hoped no one would resent her for bringing her child to the office.

She'd just convinced herself that the sooner she went inside, the sooner she could get those awkward introductions over when the door was pulled open and a fifty-something woman with an incredible bosom and flame-red hair grinned at her.

"You must be Heather," the woman said. "Jim told me you were coming, and I've been all excited at the thought of meeting you and your little girl." She took the carrier from Heather and beamed down at Diane. "Aren't you just the most precious little thing? I'm Auntie Flo and we're going to be best friends. You're even prettier than I was told, which means I'll have to have words with your uncle Jim. Yes, I will. He said beautiful, but that's not good enough. No, it's not. You're perfect. A perfect little girl."

Diane had slept through the entire introduction. Now she stirred sleepily, yawned, but didn't open her eyes.

The older woman laughed. "I guess she told me." She turned her attention to Heather and held out her hand. "I'm Flo. Welcome to Valley Helicopter. I'm delighted to have someone else in the office. It gets pretty lonely when everyone is out, and when they're in, they're too damned macho for my taste. All those pilots thinking they're God's gift to women, not to mention the repair guys in their coveralls and dirty boots. I've been telling Jim we need curtains on the windows, but what does he go buy? Mini blinds. It's not like a little gingham would've hurt anything."

Heather stared at the tall, curvy woman and hoped her mouth wasn't hanging open. Flo was unlike anyone she'd ever met. Her incredibly bright red hair was piled high on her head. She wore a tight black blouse and an even tighter black skirt, both of which showed off a womanly shape that left Heather feeling about as appealing as a stick figure. But it was Flo's conversation that was the most disconcerting.

Flo shook her hand once, then released it and grinned. "Don't pay any attention to me. I have an opinion on everything, and for the most part, I don't care if anyone agrees with me. I just like to talk. Your desk is over here.''

Still carrying Diane, Flo led the way through a medium-size office furnished with a small sofa and two straight-back chairs placed by the front desk. Behind that, a low wall with a swinging gate separated the waiting area from the rest of the room.

An executive desk sat on the left, complete with attached credenza and computer station. The surface of the desk was relatively neat, with papers stacked into impressive piles. A couple of simple metal desks stood in the center of the room.

''The pilots use those for their reports,'' Flo said. ''Or to make phone calls and stuff. You're back here.''

A doorway cut the rear wall in half. On the left side was a huge scheduling board, on the right an L-shaped desk flanked by several filing cabinets. Heather took in the computer setup, complete with printer, the neatly stacked files and a nameplate that read Heather Fitzpatrick, Senior Accountant.

''I've been promoted and it's only my first day,'' she said, confused by all that was happening.

Flo laughed. ''Jim does that all the time. He likes to make people feel important. He claims it helps with morale. I'm the office manager, if you can believe it.'' She set the baby's car seat on the desk. ''He's that kind of guy. Always thinking about his employees and wanting them to do better. He's the best boss ever. Smart, too. Not to mention good-looking. We fly some female executives and they're forever requesting him as their pilot. I swear they just want to eat him up for breakfast. But it's been a real long time since he's been interested in a woman. He's real careful before he makes a commitment.''

Heather stared into Flo's face, noting the perfect makeup that accentuated her full mouth and huge brown eyes. She supposed she could be insulted by the obvious matchmaking, but instead it made her smile. She'd been worried about being accepted by the office staff. From the looks of things, it consisted of Flo, Jim and now herself. Jim was already a friend and Flo seemed to be the kind of person who wanted to give the world a big hug.

"You're preaching to the choir," Heather said when Flo paused for breath. "I think Jim is terrific. He's a good friend and I'm lucky to have him in my life. But if you're thinking about matchmaking, I have to tell you that neither Jim nor I want that.''

Flo placed her hands on her hips. "Well, don't that beat all? Here I was so sure that boy had finally gone and fallen for someone." Her mouth twisted with regret. "Shoot. Are you sure you're just friends? He's a sexy man. I could make a lot of money selling tickets to let women stare at his butt if I could find a way to make him cooperate.''

Heather laughed. "Yes, Flo, I'm sure. Jim and I are just friends, and we both prefer it that way." She glanced around to double-check that they were alone in the office, then she lowered her voice. "However, I do agree with you about his rear end. It's pretty amazing.''

"That's something, I suppose," Flo said, but she still sounded disappointed. "Maybe I can change your mind.''

"Please don't try."

Flo's gaze turned speculative. "There must be a reason Jim wanted you around. You swear it's not personal, so I'll have to figure it out. Don't worry, I will."

Heather didn't know what to say to that.

"You probably want to get your baby settled so you can work," Flo said with a swift change of topic that left Heather feeling a little off balance. "Come on back here. I'll show you what we did to fix up a place for your baby."

Heather trailed after Flo. They left the main room and entered a short hallway.

"Bathrooms are over there," Flo said, pointing to her left. "Boys and girls. A cleaning service comes in twice a week to keep things nice. Supplies are under the sink. In that back room is a refrigerator and microwave, along with table and chairs. We have a television, but Jim doesn't like it on unless there's some big news story or a play-off game." She gave a wink. "Sports and national disasters mean we have all the boys from outside tracking dirt on our carpet."

She opened a door to the right. "This was a supply room, which is kind of a grandiose term because it's not much bigger than a closet. We put everything into two big cabinets in the lunchroom and then had this painted and fixed up for you." Flo stepped back to let her pass. "I picked out the colors myself, so I hope you like it."

Heather wasn't sure what to expect. She stepped through the doorway, turned on the light and entered baby paradise. The room was small, as Flo had said, but pale pink walls opened up the space. A crib and rocking chair in light oak took up most of the floor space. Netting acted as a shelf in a corner of the room and held nearly a dozen different stuffed animals, while teddy bears painted in pastel colors danced across two walls.

"As you can see, there wasn't much room to work with," Flo said, stepping in beside Heather. She leaned forward to unhook what looked like a shelf from the wall. "Jim came up with this idea. Sort of a fold-out changing table."

She demonstrated how to pull down the padded table. Safety bars that would keep the baby from falling snapped into place. When not in use, the entire unit could be raised and stored out of the way.

"There's a playpen in the lunchroom," Flo continued. "It's the kind that folds up flat, so we tucked it behind the door. When you want to have the baby in the office with us, we can set it up between the desks. We get a nice bit of morning sun. It's not too bright, but your daughter would probably like to play in it."

Heather took in the furniture and the decorations. Having just decorated a baby's room herself, she knew the cost and time involved. A mixture of sensations flooded through her. It was too much, and she wanted to say so, but something in her heart told her that this had been a labor of love.

"I'm overwhelmed," she admitted.

Flo picked up a teddy bear and shrugged. "I'll admit I went a little over budget, but I couldn't help myself, and Jim said he didn't care." She gave Heather a smile that didn't quite reach her eyes. "I always wanted a dozen kids of my own, but I couldn't have them. Plumbing problems. I've been spoiling my sister's kids since they were born, not to mention those in my neighborhood. So I hope you don't mind if I start right in spoiling your baby.''

Heather stared at the woman's perfect makeup, too tight clothes and tentative smile. She wondered how much pain this wonderful lady had endured in her life and how she'd come to be so strong. ''Thank you for making my baby and me feel so very welcome. I would love for you to spoil Diane as much as you'd like.''

Flo grinned. ''I might not get a lick of work done.''

They headed out to the main office. ''I'd better get her settled so I can get to work,'' Heather said, then paused. ''Would you like to put her down?''

''Thanks.'' Flo unstrapped the baby from her carrier with an expertise that told of years of practice. ''Oh, that box right there is the baby monitor. The one in her room is bolted to the wall. Just hit that pink button to turn it on.''

Heather couldn't believe all that they had done for her and was still confused as to what was going on. Little more than a month ago, she hadn't met Jim Dyer and now he'd become an important part of her life. She wasn't sure whether she should be scared or grateful. Then a soft sound came over the baby monitor. She heard Flo singing a lullaby to her daughter. Heather thought about how gentle Jim was with her child and how this job was an answer to her prayers. Obviously, after a run of bad luck where men were concerned, she'd finally started getting it right.

Jim walked into the office, a clipboard in his hand. He tossed it onto Flo's desk. ''The 197 charter is back. We're about ten hours away from an overhaul," he told her.

Flo made a note in her book. "I'll make sure it gets scheduled."

"Thanks." Jim walked to his desk and looked through the pile of messages. He couldn't actually concentrate enough to read them, but he made an attempt to act normal. He didn't want Flo to know how pleased he was that Heather had started work today.

He'd arrived long before her day had begun and he'd been out with a charter until a few minutes ago. But when he landed, he'd noticed her small, sensible sedan parked on the far side of the building, and despite the fact that he told himself they were just friends, his body had gone on major alert.

Finally, he tossed the messages onto his desk and looked at Flo. "Did Heather get here?" he asked casually.

"Don't pretend you didn't know. I heard that skip in your step when you walked into this office. She's in the nursery." She glanced at the clock on the wall. "She was feeding Diane, but they should be done now."

"I'll just go make sure she's settling in all right."

"You do that."

He ignored Flo's knowing gaze and walked toward the rear of the building. Once he entered the hall, he knocked on the door on the right. "Heather, it's Jim."

"Come on in," a soft voice called.

He pushed open the door. Heather sat in the rocking chair with Diane in her arms. The baby was upright against her shoulder, her plump pink fists resting on a towel that protected Heather's light green dress.

''We just finished our snack,'' Heather said with a smile.

She looked great. He'd seen her dozens of times in the past month, but this was the first time she'd been dressed in something more formal than leggings and a baggy T-shirt. The soft fabric of her dress draped over her body, showing the fullness of her breasts and the narrowness of her hips. She wore makeup that emphasized her green eyes and made her mouth look all pouty and tempting.

His gaze roamed over her familiar features, visiting his favorite places—her mouth, the sweep of her eyebrows, the way her hair—

''You cut your hair,'' he blurted out, noticing for the first time that the blond strands fell just to her shoulder instead of a little way down her back. She still had her bangs, but now her hair had a little wave to it as it drifted around her face. She looked mature and sophisticated in a soft and sexy kind of way.

''Do you like it?'' she asked, self-consciously touching the ends. ''I treated myself to a cut yesterday. Sort of a confidence booster before starting my new job.''

''You're beautiful,'' he said sincerely.

He told himself he wasn't supposed to notice things like that. She worked for him, they'd agreed to just be friends, and he wasn't looking to get involved. He could come up with a dozen reasons, but none of them mattered. The more time he spent with her, the more he liked her…and wanted her. Thoughts of her slender body touching his, under his and welcoming him home had kept him up for more than one night.

''Thanks.''

Diane gave a very unladylike burp, then cooed with contentment.

Heather chuckled. "Better, sweetie? You ready to say hi to your uncle Jim?" She stood up and settled the baby into his arms.

He adjusted her with an ease born of practice, then touched her soft nose. "How's my best girl?" Bright blue eyes stared up at him. He tickled her tummy. "Are you happy? Do you like coming to work with your mom?"

"How could she not?" Heather asked. "If I'd known this was what you planned when you said I could bring Diane with me—"

"What would you have done?" he asked, interrupting her. "I want you to be comfortable here."

"You went overboard."

"Don't look at me. Flo did most of the work."

"Then she did too much and you paid too much."

"When Diane doesn't need it anymore, I'll donate it to a women's shelter. Don't worry about it." He saw the questions in her eyes, questions and concerns about his real motives. He wanted to reassure her. "I did this because I wanted to. It makes me happy," he said.

"Why don't I believe you?"

"Because you're naturally suspicious. I, on the other hand, am an open and trusting person."

She smiled. "Yeah, right. We all believe that."

"My other employees would. Just ask them."

She gave him a skeptical glance but didn't pursue the subject.

"Are you getting settled?" he asked. "Finding everything?"

"Yes. Flo's been very helpful."

Jim nodded. "I knew she would be. My accountant should be here in about an hour. He'll go over the computer system with you and explain how he wants things done. You should be up and running with the books fairly quickly." He glanced down at Diane. "I'll be in the office for the rest of the afternoon so don't worry about this one. If she gets fussy, I'll take care of her."

"Gee, Flo said the same thing. I guess the two of you are going to have to fight over who will be looking after Diane." She tucked a strand of hair behind her ear. "I'm beginning to think she's the real reason you hired me."

He took a step back in mock dismay. "Oh, no. You've found me out."

"I thought as much." Heather then went on to make a comment about already having started reading the book on the computer program.

As he listened, he thought to himself that it would have been better if his affection for Diane was the real draw because caring about a child was relatively safe. Unfortunately, he was far more interested in her mother. He wanted Heather in ways he hadn't let himself want anyone in a long time.

Maybe it was the way they'd met. They'd formed an intimate bond before he'd had a chance to close himself off to her. He was paying the price now, allowing himself to stay in this too-small room, to be close enough to smell the scent of her body. It would have been safer and smarter to go out into the main office where an interested audience would force them to talk about business and nothing else.

"I should get started on that paperwork on my desk," he said. "Do you want me to set up the playpen for Diane?"

"No, she was up most of the morning, so she needs another nap. I'll settle her down. You go on."

But it was surprisingly difficult to leave the room, and even after he returned to his desk and stared at the work in front of him, he couldn't stop thinking about Heather and how dangerous it would be for her if they were ever to get involved.

Friday morning, Heather showed up with doughnuts. She took two dozen out to the hangar and left them there for the guys, then brought half a dozen inside to share with Flo and Jim.

Flo had just finished brewing coffee, and when she saw the pink box she made a low moan in her throat. "Oh, God, and I was doing so good on my diet, too."

"I'm sorry," Heather said quickly. "Let me take them outside to the guys. Just pretend you never saw them."

Flo took the box from her and clutched it to her chest. "Take these away from me and I'll be forced to kill you." She sighed again, then lifted the lid. "Oh, chocolate and jelly doughnuts." She winked at Heather. "I might need a few minutes alone with these two. If it gets too embarrassing for you, feel free to step into the other room."

Heather laughed. "Go on and have your fun. I'll take Diane back to her room."

Her baby had been up since five so she was content to relax in the now familiar crib. Heather wound up a music box, pulled up the blanket and patted Diane's tummy.

"Just squawk if you need anything, sweetie," she said as she turned on the baby monitor. "Auntie Flo will be in here before you can draw a second breath."

"I can hear you, you know," Flo called from the other room.

"I thought you were busy ingesting sugar."

"I am. Grab a cup of coffee on your way out and join me."

Heather did as she suggested and took the chair next to Flo's desk and sipped her coffee. Flo was still in raptures over the doughnuts.

"I'm only going to eat two," she promised. "If you see me lurking near the box, you have permission to drag me away, by the hair if necessary. You'll have to protect me from myself."

"Why are you on a diet?" Heather asked. "You look terrific."

Flo rolled her eyes. "This from a perfect size two."

"I'm not a size two." But she was a size four, which she figured Flo didn't want to know. "You do look great," she insisted. "I wish I were more like you and had some curves. I've been skinny my whole life. I have no muscle tone, my arms and legs look like sticks. I hate wearing a bathing suit because I don't have much on top. What I have now is because I'm breast-feeding, and that'll be gone before I know it."

Flo wore her usual tight clothing. Today it was a magenta blouse tucked into black slacks. She licked the sugar off her fingers. "I'm not feeling the least bit sympathetic, but it does my heart good to hear you complain about your body. The same body I consider amazing.''

''Do you know what it's like to have trouble filling an A-cup bra, let alone spilling out of it?''

''That's nothing.'' Flo dismissed her with a wave. ''I can gain ten pounds in less than two weeks. I've never had a flat stomach in my life, and if my breasts were any bigger, they would start showing up on county maps.''

Heather laughed. ''I once slept with a man who told me my hip bones were so sharp he was afraid I might impale him.''

''Really?'' Flo leaned toward her. ''I could beat that one a hundred times over, but it would make me feel good to have you win this little contest of ours, so that's just what I'm going to do.''

Heather looked at the woman who was quickly becoming her friend. ''Thank you, Flo.''

''For what?''

''Everything. You've been very kind to me.''

''I like having you around. It's been lonely being the only girl in the place.''

Heather thought about all the men who worked on the helicopters and the pilots who were in and out of the office. ''But there are so many cute guys around here. Don't you like that?''

Flo's smile faded and her brown eyes darkened with shadows. ''I'm not a huge fan of the male species. I adore Jim and would do just about anything for him. And I have a great man in my life now, but it wasn't always like that.''

She paused, and Heather didn't know what to say. They had clearly steered close to a very personal topic. While she was curious about her new friend, she didn't want to pry or intrude.

Flo must have read the uncertainty on her face because the older woman leaned over and touched her arm. "Don't worry about it. You couldn't have known about my past because we've never talked about it. I don't blurt it out to everyone, but I don't keep secrets, either."

She paused and took a sip of her coffee. "I was a battered wife," she said matter-of-factly. "My ex-husband beat me from the first night of our honeymoon until I left him nearly twenty-five years later."

Heather gave an involuntary start of surprise.

Flo looked at her and smiled sadly. "I know what you're thinking. Why on earth did I stay with him for twenty-five years?" She shrugged. "At the time, I could've given you a list of reasons. I didn't have any skills. He hadn't let me get a job or even have friends. I was very isolated and lived in fear for my life. But now, when I look at how horrible things were then and how far I've come, I can't believe it took me so long to get myself to a place where I had the courage to leave."

"I'm not judging you," Heather said quickly.

"I know. I appreciate your concern. To be honest, I feel like that was a lifetime ago. Maybe it was. But one night, I figured I would rather leave and risk him coming after me with a shotgun than stay and take one more slap to the face or punch to the ribs."

She pressed her full lips together. "Earlier, I said I couldn't have children because there was something wrong with my plumbing. That's only half the truth. I was fine before I got married. One night, he got it in his mind that I'd been flirting with one of my friends. I was pregnant at the time, about four months along. I'd barely talked to the man, of course, but my husband was too drunk or jealous or just looking for an excuse. He started screaming that the baby wasn't his and he was going to make me pay for that. So he started in on me, this time kicking as well as hitting. He made me lose the baby and messed me up so bad inside that I couldn't have any more children.''

Heather felt her throat tightening. ''I'm so sorry,'' she said, knowing the words were inadequate compared with her pain.

''Thank you.'' Flo leaned back in her chair. ''So I finally gathered up my courage and left. Turns out courage was all I got to take with me. He burned everything else of mine. There I was. Forty-eight years old. Never held a job. I didn't even know how to fill out an application. I was beat up, and once I hit forty, it took a lot longer for the bruises to fade. But I was determined, and I kept going out on job interviews. As expected, I wasn't successful. Until Jim Dyer gave me a chance.''

She smiled at the memory. ''At the time I didn't know a helicopter from a taxicab. He was patient and kind. He even found me a place to stay for a few months until I could save enough to move out on my own. Now I have a condo I bought myself, I'm halfway through college and I have Arnie, who's a decent guy. It's taken me a long time to get here, but I made the journey. I survived.''

''You did more than that,'' Heather said. ''You thrived.''

''Some days I would agree with you,'' Flo admitted. She jerked her head toward the window. "But I'm sure you can understand why working with a bunch of good-looking guys doesn't do much for me. I trust some of them. Jim, of course. He's a wonderful man. One day, my ex showed up here. He was determined to bring me home. Jim took him out back and gave him a lesson in what it felt like to be worked over." She smiled. "I never saw that sorry excuse for a man again."

Heather remembered Jim's offer to go after the father of her baby for abandoning her. "He has high standards for male behavior," she said.

"That he does. Jim is about the best human being on the planet." She shook her head, then sniffed. "Well, shoot. I hate starting the day on a down note. I think I need a few minutes of cuddling your beautiful baby to set my spirits to rights again. I'll be back."

Flo rose and headed for the nursery. Heather stared after her, then found her gaze drifting toward the windows. She could see several men standing around one of the helicopters. Jim was easy to spot.

She thought about what Flo had said about him and what she knew to be true. Was he a real, live hero? Heather wanted to believe that, but she wasn't sure heroes existed in real life. What was she supposed to think of a man who seemed too good to be true?

Chapter Six

Heather entered the information for the last invoice, then hit the print button. Next to her, the laser printer quietly hummed to life as three copies of the single-page document appeared in the tray. She fed in an envelope next, then collected the papers to process them.

It was late in the day, nearly six, and almost everyone had gone home. Jim still worked at his desk, but Flo had left at four-thirty as had most of the service crew outside. There weren't any night charters and no whine of helicopter rotors broke the quiet of the early evening.

As much as Heather liked coming in early and getting her work done by midafternoon, there was something to be said for the peacefulness after nearly everyone had left for home. She glanced over at Jim, but he was reading a report and didn't seem to notice her. His face was strong, his mouth firm—there wasn't even a hint of his dimple tonight. She knew if she said his name, he would look up and smile. She almost did it just to have him look at her. But that would be silly.

She returned her attention to the stack of invoices in front of her that needed to be filed. She stretched before getting up. The past couple of nights had been difficult. Diane hadn't been sleeping well and Heather couldn't figure out the reason. They'd both been up pacing for several hours, and more than ever, Heather had appreciated her flexible hours. When Diane finally fell asleep at five in the morning, Heather had been able to climb back in bed, too, without having to worry about getting to her job first thing.

"Where's the book on number twenty-seven?" Jim asked without removing his gaze from the report.

Heather stood up, collected the three-ring binder containing all the service records for that particular helicopter and handed it to him.

"Thanks," he said.

She returned to her desk, picked up the pile of invoices and walked over to the filing cabinets. Moving around eased some of the cricks out of her back. She still wasn't used to long hours at a computer or being tired all the time. Even with her flexible schedule, she was at the mercy of a baby who didn't understand that Mommy was dying for eight uninterrupted hours of sleep.

Heather opened the file drawer and organized the invoices by number. She found it hard to concentrate, and while she wanted to explain the phenomenon away as latent hormones or sleep deprivation, she knew it had a lot more to do with the man sitting at the other end of the office.

Just thinking about him made her stomach flutter. She had to force herself not to make excuses to talk to him during the day, and when they were together, she wanted to beg him to touch her. Nothing wild or sexual, just a little pat on the arm or the shoulder or the rear.

That last image made her grin. She was a bad girl and she had it for him in a bad way. The excuse that it was just hormones was wearing thin. Diane was nearly two months old. Surely Heather's body was well on the mend and her glands were easing their pregnancy vigil. Maybe it was—

The front door of the office opened and an attractive young couple stepped into the waiting area. The man was of medium height with black hair and brown eyes, in his mid- to late-twenties. The woman was petite and shared his warm coloring. Jim glanced up and grinned. "Rick! What are you doing here?" He rose to his feet and headed over to the couple.

"I wanted to see you," Rick said as he and his companion stepped through the swinging gate. The two men shook hands warmly, then Rick nodded at the young woman beside him. "You remember Lupe, don't you?" His smile broadened. "She's my woman."

"Rick!" Lupe blushed. "I'm very happy to see you again, Mr. Dyer."

"Call me Jim," he said. "It's good to see you, too." His gaze dropped to her left hand. "Nice ring. I see you finally let Rick convince you to take a

chance on him. I don't think you'll be disappointed.
He's a good man." He slapped Rick on the back. "A
bit of a slow learner at times, but he finally figured
out what was right."

"Thanks to you," Lupe said.

Jim shrugged off the compliment. "He did all the
hard work. I just showed him a couple of unpleasant
alternatives if he kept messing up. But that's all in
the past. Rick, Lupe, I want you to meet my new
bookkeeper and very good friend."

Heather had been filing invoices, and although she
was trying not to listen, it was difficult when they
were standing only a few feet behind her. Now she
turned toward the group.

"Heather, this is Rick Martinez. He worked for me
until about six months ago. And this is his fiancée,
Lupe."

"Nice to meet you both," Heather said.

"Have a seat," Jim told them. "Tell me what's
going on."

Heather dropped the last invoice in the filing cab-
inet. "This is a private conversation," she said. "I
don't want to interrupt. I'll just get my stuff and head
on home."

"Don't go," Jim insisted, herding her back to his
desk. He motioned for Rick to pull up a couple more
chairs, then grabbed one for Heather. "We're all
friends here."

Heather stared at him helplessly. She wasn't completely comfortable joining people who had obviously
known each other a long time, but she also didn't
want to appear rude by leaving. She decided she

would stay for a few minutes, then make her excuses and go.

Jim settled into his seat behind his desk. "Tell me how you're doing, Rick. How's the new job working out?"

"Great." Rick moved his chair closer to Lupe, then took her hand and threaded his fingers through hers. "I'm getting advanced training with the helicopters and they're sending me to a management seminar in the fall. It's two nights a week and everyone says it's tough, but I think I'll be okay."

He sounded modest, but Heather saw the pride and pleasure glowing in his large, dark eyes.

"If I get through the class and do well, they want to promote me." He grinned. "I never saw myself as one of the suits."

Jim motioned to his own casual long-sleeved shirt and khakis. "This is hardly a suit, but I think you'll do great in management. You have a lot of the traits needed. I'm sure you'll find the class interesting but not as hard as you think."

Lupe turned her shy gaze on Jim. "We're getting married next month."

"Yeah, man," Rick said. "How come you didn't accept the invitation?"

Jim frowned. "I thought I sent my reply." He dug around in a couple of stacks of paper on his desk, then withdrew an ivory envelope and handed it to Rick. "Here, take it with you and use the postage for something else."

Rick's gaze was direct. "You're really going to come?"

"I wouldn't miss it for the world."

Rick glanced at Heather. "You can bring a date if you want."

"I just might do that."

Rick turned his full attention on her. "How long have you worked for this guy?" he asked.

Heather's mind was still on the "bring a date" comment and she wondered who Jim might bring. From what she'd heard, he didn't have a girlfriend, but maybe there was someone he saw now and then. The thought didn't set well with her.

"About three weeks," Heather said after a pause.

Rick nodded. "He's the best." He ran his fingers through his dark hair. "You probably can't tell to look at me now, but not too long ago, I was a real loser. I graduated from my technical training, but barely. I didn't care much about working. I wanted to party with my friends. Jim gave me a job, then I gave him hell for months." He looked at his former boss. "Remember?"

"You were a real pain in the butt."

Rick laughed. "I was late. I came to work drunk." He squeezed Lupe's hand. His humor faded. "She left me and Jim fired me, all on the same day. About a week later, Jim came to see me and took me on a little field trip."

"To the county jail," Jim said softly.

Heather stiffened in her seat. "Why?"

"To show me where I was headed," Rick answered. "Guys from the neighborhood had been to jail and they said it was no big deal. They came back with tattoos and stories about how all their friends were there. They made it sound like a party. Jim showed me differently. Then he got me into AA and gave me back my job. Only I always had to work with one of the other guys. I couldn't even go to the bathroom by myself.''

"Whatever works," Jim said.

"I nearly quit a couple of times, but pretty soon I found out that when I got some sleep and didn't come to work drunk, I liked what I was doing and I was good at it. Lupe saw the change in me and agreed to give me another chance. After two years, Jim helped me find the job where I am now.'' He looked at his former boss. "I owe you. Anything I can ever do for you, let me know.''

Jim waved off the offer. "All I want is for you to be happy and successful.''

Conversation continued to flow around her, but Heather only listened. She was too surprised by all she'd already learned to try to participate. She knew that Jim liked to help people, but she hadn't realized how directly he'd been involved in his employees' lives. If he hadn't intervened with Rick, there was no telling where the young man might have ended up. By all accounts, he'd made a complete turnaround. Somehow Jim must have known that the young man would respond to his attempts to save him.

She heard a cry from the other room and excused herself. She was in the middle of changing Diane when there was a knock on the open door. Lupe stood there with a shy smile.

"May I see her?'' the young woman asked. She was incredibly beautiful, with huge eyes and blue-black hair that hung halfway down her back.

"Sure. This little girl has learned to thrive on attention, haven't you, sweet cheeks?'' Heather smiled when she realized that she'd started using Jim's endearment for the child. She finished securing the diaper, then snapped Diane's sleeper into place. She picked up the baby and turned her to face their visitor. "Diane, this is Lupe."

Lupe giggled and took a tentative step forward. "May I hold her?"

"Sure."

Heather settled the baby into the young woman's arms and was instantly aware that Lupe must have been around babies before.

"I have several younger brothers and sisters," Lupe said, confirming her guess. "My friends who come from large families swear they don't want many children themselves, but I do." She smiled sweetly at the baby. "You're lucky you can bring her to work with you."

"I know. Jim's a good boss."

"Oh, yes." Lupe's expression turned almost reverent. "He's done many wonderful things for Rick. We both admire him very much. He is so kind and giving."

Jim *was* darned wonderful. But while Heather wanted to believe that reality was just what it seemed, she couldn't help thinking there had to be some deep, dark secret he was hiding. No one was that good…were they?

"I think Jim is lonely," Lupe said. "He doesn't have a woman."

"Not one that we know about," Heather agreed. "That doesn't mean he doesn't have a private life. Maybe he wants to keep work and his personal world separate."

Lupe looked doubtful. "I'm not sure. I don't think he's been married."

That surprised Heather. She hadn't really thought about Jim's past, but if she had, she would have assumed that some lucky girl had snapped him up years ago. She would have guessed that the bride in question had died or something. Jim didn't seem like the kind of man a woman would easily let go. Unless the deep, dark secret was really bad. If there was a secret at all. Maybe he was exactly as wonderful as he appeared.

Lupe cooed over Diane. "She's so pretty and sweet. Rick and I want to wait a while before we start our family. He says he's making enough money so that when we get married next month, I won't have to work." She gave a little giggle of excitement. "I'm going to college. I never thought I could afford it, but Rick says we can. He's proud that I was accepted and even got a partial scholarship to the local state university. It won't be easy, but I've always wanted to get my degree."

"Sounds like the two of you have some wonderful plans. I'm sure they're all going to happen exactly as you want."

"Thank you. I hope so."

Heather had to quell a flash of envy. There had been a time when she'd been young and naive, facing a future she'd been sure was full of promise. Everything had changed, of course. But could she lay all the blame at Peter's door? Hadn't some of the fault been hers?

"Rick has proved himself to be a good man," Heather said. "When the going got tough, he didn't run away. He worked through his problems. When you two have difficulties, he'll do the same. That's what'll matter. If you are both willing to try, then you can survive anything.''

Lupe smiled, then held out her arms. ''She's fallen asleep.''

Heather laughed. ''Of course she has. It's daytime. She likes to be up at night, the little stinker.'' She took her daughter and placed her back in the crib, then smoothed the blanket over her.

Not long after the two women returned to the office, Rick and Lupe were saying goodbye. They made Jim promise to stay in touch and then they were gone. Jim looked uncomfortable as he shifted his weight from foot to foot, then cleared his throat.

''I didn't really do all that much for Rick,'' he said. ''He was basically a good kid who lost his way.''

''It sounded a little bit more than that to me,'' Heather countered.

The sun was low in the sky and light poured through the west-facing windows. Jim stood a little hunched over, with his hands in his pockets. His hair needed cutting and a five o'clock shadow darkened his jaw. He should have looked a mess. Instead, he was so good-looking, her thighs trembled.

''So am I supposed to bow when I come into the room?'' she asked teasingly. ''I've never been around a real, live hero before.''

''I'm not a hero.''

''Rick and Lupe would disagree.''

''They're just kids.''

''Out of the mouths of babes and all that,'' she persisted.

She wasn't sure why she was pushing him. It's not as if she *wanted* to know that he was incredibly special. If anything, that information would make him harder to resist. But she was getting a lot of messages from different people and they all said the same thing—that Jim Dyer wasn't like every other guy around and that she was lucky to have him in her life. Even if they were just friends.

She went to her desk and began tidying up. It was getting late and she should be heading home. But she couldn't forget what she and Lupe had talked about or what the younger woman had said about Jim's being lonely.

"Have you ever been married?" she asked suddenly.

Jim walked over to his desk and settled on a corner. Heather's question had caught him off guard. He'd expected her to ask about Rick or the other kids who worked for him, but not about his own past.

"Married?" Who would have wanted him? "No. You?"

He asked the question automatically; it was one of those social responses that seemed required. When someone asked about your weekend, you asked about his. He expected her to say she hadn't been.

"Once," she said, "a long time ago."

"You were married?" he asked without thinking.

She looked up from the papers she'd been sorting and smiled. "Don't sound so surprised. When I'm not nine months pregnant or recovering from giving birth, I clean up pretty good."

"That's not what I meant," he told her. "You're very attractive. I was expressing surprise because I didn't think any man would let you go once he'd found you.''

Her gaze narrowed. ''And here I was thinking the same thing about you,'' she said cryptically but didn't explain her remark. ''I was very young and even more foolish.'' She lowered herself into her chair. ''You sure you want to hear the story?''

''If you want to tell it.'' For him, it didn't matter what Heather talked about; he just liked listening to the sound of her voice.

''I met Peter in high school. He was a year older than me, very cute, athletic, but not much of a scholar. He was also the first guy who ever paid attention to me.'' She leaned back in her chair and smiled. ''I was not the ideal body type back then as you can imagine. I was even thinner and a little too studious to be popular.''

''I bet you had your share of guys with crushes on you,'' Jim said. If he'd known her then, he knew he would have been one of them.

She raised her eyebrows. ''If they existed, they were a very quiet and subtle group. Anyway, I fell madly in love with Peter, and when I finally graduated from high school and he wanted to get married, I said yes. I also had a partial scholarship to a state college, but it was out of town, so I had to choose.''

''You picked Peter.''

She nodded. ''My mother was heartbroken, but she didn't judge me. I can only hope I'll be as good a parent to Diane.'' She toyed with the collar of her loose-fitting white blouse. ''A few months after Peter and I got married, my mother met the man she's married to now. It was a whirlwind courtship, and before

I knew what happened, she'd moved to Florida and I was all alone. Or so it seemed.''

He didn't like listening to the story. Even though it had been years ago and had obviously ended badly, he didn't want to know that Heather had given her heart to a foolish young man. He wanted her to have always been happy.

''You had Peter.''

''Sort of,'' she agreed. ''But he wasn't ready to grow up. So while I worked two jobs to support us, Peter partied with his friends and dreamed about playing football for the local community college. He didn't want to take classes. He just wanted to play ball.'' She drew in a deep breath as if preparing herself for what happened next.

''One day, when we'd been married for about three years, I came home early from work and found Peter in bed with a high school cheerleader. I packed my bags and vowed that I would learn from the experience.''

''I'm sorry.''

''Thanks, but as I said, it was a long time ago and I'm fine with it. I'm not bitter about Peter. He was too young to make a marriage work. I probably was, too.''

''At least you wanted to try.''

''Trying wasn't enough. Maybe I wanted too much. Maybe all I could see was that someone other than my mother finally loved me. Or so it seemed.''

''You'd been lonely,'' he said.

''A little. Maybe more than a little.''

He'd been lonely, too, he thought. He knew what it was like to fall in love in high school, to be willing to give up anything for that love, then have the gift thrown back in his face.

"So I've learned my lesson about love," she said.

"What's the lesson?"

"I don't go there anymore. While love seems to work out for other people, it's not in the cards for me."

"You're being a little hasty making that decision after one failure."

She shook her head. "You're forgetting the ever gracious Luke, who abandoned both me and his child."

"You're right." He clenched his hands into fists. "Okay, two lessons."

She held up three fingers. "Three lessons. In between Peter and Luke, I fell for another guy. Once again, I was working two jobs, and I met a great guy who seemed to be everything Peter hadn't been—mature, motivated, a hard worker."

"He sounds perfect," Jim grumbled.

"Yes, he does. After two years of dating, he still couldn't bring himself to commit to anything permanent. We were stuck in the dating mode. So I gave him an ultimatum. Propose or it's over."

"What happened?" he asked although he already knew.

"He left. Six week later, I heard that he'd met a woman and moved in with her. Three months after that, they were married. Apparently, his problem wasn't with commitment, but with me. Which was why Luke seemed so perfect. All he talked about was getting married. Of course, he already had a wife, but I didn't know that."

Jim wanted to pull Heather close until all the hurt was gone. But he didn't...for two reasons. First, she wouldn't understand what he was doing and might think he was coming on to her. Second, the hurt *was* gone. Despite the setbacks in her life, she'd managed to heal herself. She had a strength and self-reliance that he admired.

"What happens now?" he asked.

She shrugged. "Now I'm grateful I have a wonderful daughter to raise. My goal will be to follow in my mother's footsteps."

"You're too young and have too much to offer to stay single for long. You deserve more," Jim said.

If he didn't let himself think about the possibility of Heather with another man, he could actually believe what he was saying.

"I could say that you deserve more, too," she told him. "But if the rumors are to be believed, you live like a monk."

"That's a slight exaggeration. I have female friends, but I prefer to keep things light. I'm not looking for emotional commitment." He'd explained his position enough times that he could say the words easily, without even having to think about why he'd chosen to do without what most men considered a given—a wife and a family.

"To throw your own words back in your face," she said, "you're too young and you have too much to offer for you to stay single for long."

"It's worked so far."

Her gaze settled on his face. "I'm guessing that there are several broken hearts littering the ground. So I can't help wondering why you're avoiding any

serious romantic entanglement. I mean, it makes sense
for me. Three strikes and all that. But what's your
excuse?''

''I don't want anyone getting hurt.''

''That sounds like a lonely way to live.''

''You're not in a position to cast stones, Heather,''
he said gently. ''You're lonely, too.''

She nodded. ''You're right. We're in the same position, which is probably why we get along so well.''
She stood up and grinned at him. ''All right. Enough
of this philosophizing. I'm collecting my daughter
and heading home. You want to join us for dinner?''

''I can't, but thanks for asking.''

''Sure.''

She moved into the hallway, then disappeared into
Diane's room. Jim watched her go, taking in the long
navy skirt that outlined her slender hips and the way
those hips swayed with every step. His need for her
was growing. He would have sold his soul to join
Heather for dinner tonight, but he couldn't. Because
he would be taking a chance. The first week of their
acquaintance, he'd decided to only be around her
when he was feeling strong and could resist doing all
those things he wanted. In time, he would teach himself to be happy and content with the crumbs available to him. But not yet. And until he was accepting
of just her friendship, he would do whatever he had
to to keep them both safe from potential disaster.

Chapter Seven

"I've got to get these to the Federal Express drop-off box before they pick up today," Flo said as she paused by Heather's desk. "If he finishes what he's doing—" she nodded her head toward the teenage boy filling out an employment application "—go ahead and take it from him, then have him wait until Jim gets back. Shouldn't be more than a couple of minutes."

"No problem," Heather told her.

Flo headed for the front door, slapped herself on the forehead, then turned to face Heather again. "Did you confirm the cake?"

"Yes. We're all set."

"You told me that an hour ago, didn't you?" Flo sighed. "I swear, I'm becoming more forgetful with each passing minute. Soon I'll need to wear a name

tag just so I remember who I am. Back in a second.''
With that, she pushed her way through the door.

It was tough to believe, but Heather had been working for Jim for five weeks. Time was flying by. Jim liked to tease her that Diane would soon be driving. While her baby was growing fast, Heather knew she had a little bit of time until extra car insurance was an issue in her life. After all, Diane was only ten weeks old.

Ten weeks. Was that how long she'd known Jim? It felt longer to her, but in a good way. He'd accepted her into his business with a trust that made her want to work even harder than she normally did. His employees were friendly and open; Flo had become a close friend. The business was oddly like an extended family where everyone knew everyone else and cared about what happened.

There were some exceptions, of course. Charter pilots who breezed through on a regular basis didn't always want to participate in the camaraderie. Most of them were employed by companies who simply leased equipment from Valley Helicopter Services. Heather had gotten to know a few of their names, but little else. Yet with the regular employees, it was different. She'd overheard conversations about helping a work buddy move, stock tips and offers of a ride home when required. She'd also found out they all had something in common—at one time or another they'd needed help and Jim had been there.

Heather had come to grips with the fact that he'd seen her as just another stray who needed rescuing. Since their first meeting, they'd formed a friendship, but even he had admitted that his initial impression of her had been that of a brand-new mother who was unlikely to make it on her own.

At first his confession had annoyed her, and she'd taken great pains to inform him that she had been fine before she met him and she would still be fine if their paths had never crossed. But then she'd remembered that this was Jim—he couldn't help himself. He was a born fixer by nature, and if he saw a problem he had to step in and do something about it. As far as flaws went, it wasn't a bad one.

So here she was, employed in an office of misfits. The irony was, of course, that instead of feeling out of place, she felt as if she'd found a second home. Frankly, she couldn't think of a better place to work.

"Excuse me," the young man said.

Heather glanced up and saw the teenager standing by her desk. "Yes?"

"I've finished my application."

He was tall and very thin, with too long brown hair and big brown eyes. He wore a button-down shirt with freshly pressed khakis. Probably the best clothing he owned, Heather thought as she glanced at the sheet of paper in front of her. "Thanks—" she looked at the name on the application "—thanks, Brian. Have a seat in the waiting area. Jim should be back in a few minutes."

"Okay." The kid tried to smile but failed. He also didn't move from the side of her desk. "I'm only seventeen," he said. "My birthday was last week. I came here when I turned sixteen, but Mr. Dyer said I had to wait another year. So I'm back."

"You must really want to work here," Heather said.

Brian nodded so hard his bangs fell across his fore-head and into his eyes. He pushed them back in an impatient gesture. "I want to learn to fly helicopters. I know that's not part of the job," he added hastily, "but I want to learn about 'em, be close to 'em, you know?"

"I think I understand." He was so young and so earnest, Heather thought.

"I mostly need the money, but I thought maybe by working here I could learn something useful for later." His eager expression clouded. "But there's probably a ton of guys waiting to work here and I guess they have more experience than me. I don't guess Mr. Dyer is going to want to hire me."

Heather wasn't so sure, but she didn't want to say anything to get Brian's hopes up. She hadn't even known that Jim was looking to hire someone, so she didn't know about the other applicants.

Before she could think of an appropriate response, Diane started to cry. Heather excused herself and went into the nursery to collect her daughter. Diane quieted as soon as she saw her. Heather scooped her up, then felt her diaper.

"You're just a faker," she said softly. "You're dry, and you ate less than an hour ago, so I know you're not hungry. You want some attention, don't you?"

Big blue eyes stared at her face.

"Just as I thought," Heather murmured. "It's all about you, huh?" She laughed, then kissed her daughter's forehead. "Fine. You can have as much attention as you want. Let's go back to the office."

Carrying Diane, she returned to her desk. Brian was

still standing beside it. When he saw the baby, he smiled.

"My sister just had a boy. I'm going to teach him how to play baseball."

"Probably not for a couple of weeks at least," Heather teased.

Brian blushed. "No, ma'am. He'll need to be a lot older than he is now. I wasn't sure about having a baby around, but he's pretty cool. I go visit him a lot."

She liked this young man, Heather thought as she glanced out the window and saw Jim heading toward the office. He seemed intelligent and sincere.

The front door opened. Brian spun around, saw Jim and stiffened. "Hello, Mr. Dyer. I don't know if you remember me. I'm Brian Johnson. I was here last year about a job and you said to wait until I was seventeen."

Jim looked the teenager over. "When was your birthday?"

"Last week. But I had family commitments until this morning, so this is the soonest I could get here."

Jim nodded, then gave Heather a wink. "Why don't you grab your application, Brian? We'll take a walk around the place while we talk about things."

Brian turned back to her. "Thank you for listening to me, ma'am."

"You're welcome. Good luck."

But Heather wasn't sure the young man was going to need it. Jim had that look in his eye. The one that told her he was planning to give a seventeen-year-old kid a chance to make his dreams come true.

"Everything ready for the party?" Jim asked as Brian stepped outside.

"Of course," Heather said. "You and Flo both worry too much."

"At least I'm in good company." He gave her a brief wave, then disappeared outside.

Fifteen minutes later, she had Diane strapped into her baby carrier and was helping Flo set out paper plates and napkins. They were using part of the main hangar for their party. One section at the side of the open space had been walled off and filled with tables and chairs. Jim held his meetings with employees out here. The plain room had been brightened with crepe paper and colorful balloons hanging from the low ceiling and tied to the backs of chairs.

"Harry's bringing the ice," Flo said as she pointed to the empty metal container on the floor. It looked big enough to serve as a tub for a Great Dane. "Jim says soft drinks only for this kind of party, and I've always agreed with him. Alcohol and helicopters don't mix."

As usual, Flo was dressed to inspire. Electric-blue slacks clung to round hips, while a black T-shirt emphasized her impressive bosom.

"Now where are the forks?" Flo searched through the cabinets lining the wall and finally found a large bag filled with plastic forks. "We have plates, napkins, forks, a cutting knife and an ice-cream scoop." She shuddered. "I'll let you handle the ice cream. Sodas are on their way along with the ice, so I think that's everything."

"Why is Mark leaving?" Heather asked as she checked on her daughter. Diane clutched her small cloth bunny to her chest and occasionally chewed on its ear. "Every time we talked, he seemed very happy with his job."

"Oh, he is." Flo pulled out one of the metal folding chairs and plopped down. "But Jim got him a job with a bigger company—one that has room for advancement."

That sounded familiar, Heather thought. "He did the same thing for Rick Martinez a few months back, didn't he?"

Flo looked surprised. "How'd you hear about that?"

Heather told her about the young couple's visit and all that Rick and Lupe had said about Jim.

"Well, it's all true," Flo told her. "He's one of the few businesses in the area that's willing to hire people directly out of a trade school. It's the old problem of needing experience to get a job and needing a job to get experience. He gives them experience, then finds them better jobs. Then a whole new batch of graduates comes through and he does the same for them."

Heather wasn't sure how she felt about that. "But he has to do a lot of extra work that way," she said. "All that training of new people. Who can he depend on?"

"A few of the guys stick around despite Jim's attempts to move them somewhere else. He's been trying to get rid of me for years, but I haven't budged."

None of this made sense to Heather. "I'm still confused. What does he get out of it?"

Flo's expression was unreadable. "He likes to help people, but I also think..." Her voice trailed off.

"Well, it's just my theory. If you want to know, I guess you'll have to ask him yourself."

"How long *have* you worked here?"

"Six years. Sometimes I make Jim crazy because he finds me these terrific jobs and I turn them all down. But I've told him I'm not going anywhere until I'm ready. He doesn't get to set my timetable. If he's unhappy with my work, he can fire me, of course."

"Flo, he adores you and you do a terrific job. He would never fire you."

The older woman winked. "I know. So he's stuck with me."

Heather stroked her daughter's cheek. She had the feeling that she'd just been given an important piece of information. That if she could put it all together, she would have learned something important about Jim. The problem was that she couldn't get the pieces to fit yet.

Jim liked to hire people, train them and then move them on. What did that mean? That he was a fool? Or a hero? Everybody adored Jim, but how did Jim feel about everyone else? Was there still a deep, dark secret, or was she looking for monsters under her bed? Monsters that existed only in her mind?

Jim walked into the hangar close to six. The party was in full swing. He could hear music blaring and the sounds of conversation and laughter. The place was jammed because most of the employees came to the going-away parties. Even the charter pilots stopped by if they were in the area.

He waved to several of the maintenance guys but found his gaze relentlessly searching the room until he'd found what he was looking for. Heather stood with her back to him, talking to Harry.

She'd kept her hair short, the layered cut falling just to her shoulders. While he'd liked the longer length, he had to admit this style was very flattering. Even from behind, he could see how the blond strands moved with her and caught the light. She wore tailored slacks and a long-sleeved pink blouse. Her hips were narrow, her legs long. Over the past few weeks, the last traces of her pregnancy had faded, leaving her looking lean and trim.

If the truth were told, she was a little thinner than he usually liked his women. In the past, he'd been a fan of curves. While Flo was a little older and not his type, he'd always admired her figure. But Heather's leanness was growing on him. Besides, she was more than just a body. With her, he wanted the whole package.

She touched Harry's arm, then turned and spotted him. Instantly, her face lit up in a smile. Jim told himself not to read too much into that. That it didn't mean anything. But he couldn't help responding in kind, knowing that anyone watching him would be able to figure out that he had it bad for this woman.

"You're here," Heather said. "We were beginning to wonder."

"I wouldn't have missed it," he told her, then glanced at her plate. He raised his eyebrows. "Two pieces of cake."

"Uh-huh." She licked her fork.

"I thought women were always on a diet."

"Not me. I have one of those bodies that won't let me put on weight. Which isn't as pleasant as it sounds. I've looked like a waif all my life and I've never had breasts.'' She glanced down at her chest. ''Except now that I'm breast-feeding.''

Jim found his gaze straying to her chest even as he told himself he should turn away. Heather was slight, but her torso was just shapely enough to be interesting.

''How did it go with Brian?'' she asked, bringing him back to earth with a thump.

''The interview was good. He's a bright kid, and motivated. His father ran out on the family about three years ago and rarely makes an appearance. His mom works hard and isn't around much. His older sister takes up the slack, but she's got a husband and a new baby, so Brian's not getting the attention he needs, nor does he have a male role model in his life.''

''So you're going to hire him.'' It wasn't a question.

He nodded. ''At first he'll just clean up around the place. Wash down the helicopters, that sort of thing. But I'll work with him myself. He's smart and he'll pick things up quickly. He's starting his senior year of high school in September. He doesn't have a lot of money for college, but if things work out here, I know people who can help.''

He stopped talking when he realized Heather was staring at him with a strange look on her face. She'd paused with her fork halfway to her mouth and was looking at him.

''What?'' he asked.

She shrugged. ''You're into misfits,'' she said. ''People who are lost. You take them in and fix them.

Then—'' she pointed to the party going on around them ''—when they're all better, you send them on their way.''

It hadn't taken her very long to figure him out. He wasn't sure if he was annoyed or relieved. ''And if I do?''

''Why?'' she asked. ''Why do you do it?''

There was no way to answer that question truthfully. No one really knew what was in it for him. If they did, they would be shocked. He didn't want to see that look of disgust on Heather's face. So he talked around the truth, getting close to it without actually having to say it.

''I like helping people,'' he said. ''I'm in a position where I can, so I do. I like getting people to a better place in their lives. I want to give back.''

''Hmm.'' She didn't sound convinced. ''I suspect there's more to it.''

There was. The wide circle of people around him allowed him to continue in the illusion that he had a place to belong, that there were caring individuals in his life. The reality was he moved them along before they had the chance to get too close and figure out the truth.

''I want to believe you,'' she said. ''I want to believe that you're one of the good guys, but I've spent my life being around men who were decent on the surface and lousy underneath. I don't want to make that mistake again.''

She stared up at him with a damned earnest expression on her face. God, she was so beautiful with her big eyes and tempting mouth. He wanted to kiss her right there in front of everyone. But he didn't. If he ever kissed Heather, he wanted it to be in private. Not like this.

Instead he touched her cheek. "I'm not one of the good guys or bad guys. I'm just a man. I have things I like about myself and things I want to change."

"You make it sound so simple."

Her skin was like silk against his fingers and he wanted to discover every curve. But this wasn't the time. He lowered his hand to his side, then shoved it into his jeans pocket. "It is simple," he told her. "I know you've had some bad experiences, but there are more men in the world than those three."

She didn't look convinced. "Can you give me a list of names and phone numbers? I want to meet these regular guys myself. Not that I don't trust your judgment."

"But you don't," he said.

"Not really." She smiled. "Actually, I do trust you, but your criteria for a good man are probably different from mine. Men get weird when women are involved. Not to mention sex."

They were alone in a crowded room. Jim had heard that phrase before, but he'd never experienced it until this moment. Despite the conversation and music flowing around them, he could only see Heather.

Her gaze held his and he wanted to believe he saw desire there—a flame that matched his own. But he wasn't sure. Besides, they'd agreed to keep it simple. She was bright and funny and pretty and he was terrified she was going to find out the truth about him. He could understand why he wanted her—what man wouldn't?—but what would she see in him?

"I still can't decide about you," she said. "If you

are a real, live hero, I might have to rethink my opinion of men. Although I'm not thrilled with being someone's charity case.''

''You were never that.'' He touched her arm, trying to ignore the warmth of her and the softness of her skin and the feel of her blouse against his fingers. ''I admire your spirit. You're strong and brave and devoted to your daughter. You've also done a great job at planning your life.''

She grinned. ''Gee, don't you think a decent grizzly bear mom would have all those same characteristics? Well, not the planning part, but the rest of it. Of course I'm devoted. I love Diane with my whole heart and I'm lucky to have my mother as a role model on how to be a single parent. I'm not so sure about brave. Maybe stubborn would be a better description.''

''Whatever works,'' he said.

She nodded her agreement. ''As for planning my life, I'll have to disagree with you on that. If I'd planned better, I probably wouldn't have gotten involved with those three men in my life. Except if I hadn't met Luke, I wouldn't have Diane. In my opinion, it was worth it to deal with him because I got her.'' She nibbled on her cake. ''It's one of those time-and-space paradoxes that can't be explained.''

''I was referring to the plans you made since finding out you were pregnant. You've worked with a potentially difficult situation and made the best of it.''

''Thanks.'' Her smile made her eyes crinkle at the corners. ''I've learned from the best.''

''I admire you.'' He said the words without thinking, then figured she wouldn't understand what he really meant, so it was safe.

Her grin broadened. "Okay. I'll be your hero if you'll be mine."

"I'm not hero material. Wish I were."

"Sorry, Jim, but you're outvoted. And if you don't believe me, I'd be happy to take an informal poll in this very room."

She motioned to the party in progress around them, and he didn't have any choice but to agree with her and let it go. No one here knew the truth except maybe Flo, who might have guessed it. So he changed the subject and they ended up talking about work. Then Harry and Flo joined them, and his few moments alone with Heather were gone.

He watched her as she talked with different people, watched the way the fading sunlight played on her hair and how she would excuse herself to check on Diane who was sleeping in a quiet alcove in the hangar. He thought about how much he'd grown to want her, how the wanting was painful at times, and yet he wouldn't change it for the world. When he wanted Heather, he felt that he was still alive, that he was connecting with another human being. With her around, he could pretend the world wasn't so very empty.

He could want her and even need her, but he had to stop short of caring for her. He alone knew the price of that and it was one place he was never going to go to again.

Chapter Eight

"This is never going to work!" Heather said with a laugh as her lovely daughter completely ignored the photographer frantically waving a stuffed bear.

"Of course it will work," Jim told her seriously. "Diane is being a little coy because she knows she's the prettiest baby here and she doesn't want to give anything away, but she'll come around."

"You're crazy. I love my child and I think she's brilliant, but she's not even three months old. There's no way she's capable of thinking such complex thoughts."

Although when Diane happened to glance at her, a serious and thoughtful expression on her face, Heather suddenly wondered if Jim was right.

"Maybe she hates being dressed like a rabbit," she said. After Diane had been photographed wearing a pink dress, they'd put her in a little bunny costume.

"It's not that," Jim said confidently, as if he and Diane had chatted on this very topic.

"Come on, Diane," the young male photographer urged as he continued to wave the toy in the air. "Look at the camera and smile so Mommy can have a nice picture of you. Come on."

Diane sat propped up against a pile of powder-blue pillows in front of a backdrop painted to look like puffy white clouds and a broad expanse of sky. She wore the terry-cloth bunny jacket and hat with great style, but she didn't seem the least bit interested in having her picture taken.

Heather leaned against the front counter and figured she'd have to step in herself at some point to see if she could get Diane to look toward the camera.

"Are you glad you're doing this?" Jim asked.

"Actually, I am."

He'd asked her help in picking out a wedding present for Rick and Lupe, then had suggested that they stop by the department-store photographer so that Heather could have pictures taken of Diane. It was, he told her very seriously, important to have a record of her daughter's changes over the months. Heather hadn't had the heart to tell him that she already had dozens of photos at home. However, the idea of a more professional photograph had been appealing. She could pick out a couple of different poses and send them along to her mother.

"Come on, Diane," the photographer coaxed once more.

Diane seemed fascinated by a loose thread on one of the pillows.

"I'll fix this," Jim said in that tone of voice that

announced he was a man about to solve an important problem. Women and children should step aside.

Heather did just that. Jim moved to the box of toys and picked out a stuffed purple puppy. He shook it a couple of times as if checking the flexibility of the animal, then walked toward Diane. He crouched down and checked to make sure he wasn't in the way of the camera.

"Hi there, sweet cheeks."

Diane turned toward the sound of his voice and gave him her best toothless grin. Her entire face lit up, her little eyes scrunching together and her hands waving in delight.

"Got it," the photographer said as the camera flashed several times in a row. "Just a couple more."

"You want a puppy?" Jim asked, holding up the stuffed animal. "Can you say puppy?"

Diane's expression remained thrilled. She was getting attention from the favorite guy in her life. Heather watched her daughter and realized the situation had just gotten more complicated. It had probably been that way all along, but she hadn't been aware of it. Here she was trying to keep the possibly perfect Jim Dyer at arm's length while not noticing how her daughter had bonded with him. In Diane's very simple world, Jim fulfilled all the functions of a father.

Heather reacted first with panic, then forced herself to stay calm. She didn't have to change anything just yet. Jim was great with her daughter, and until she found a reason to worry, she should just be happy that her child was surrounded by people who adored her.

Her own concerns were different. Because she was

an adult, her relationship with him was more complicated…especially because she still couldn't find any serious flaws in his character. Even so, she couldn't escape the suspicion that he was hiding something pretty big. What was it? Had he robbed banks in his youth? Did he practice extortion? There had to be something because no one was that good.

"That should do it," the photographer said. "You can pick the pictures up in ten days."

"Thanks," Heather said, but made no move to collect Diane. Jim was already taking care of that, first removing her costume, then holding her close.

"You were brilliant," he told the infant as he cradled her in his arms before setting her into the stroller and carefully securing her in place. "Very lovely. The pictures will be beautiful because you're beautiful. Yes, you are. And smart and fun. Did I mention you were my favorite little girl in the whole world?"

He straightened and gave Heather a quick smile. "She says she's ready to go, but she wants us to leave via the toy department."

Heather settled her purse strap over her shoulder and motioned for Jim to push the stroller. "She did not say that. You said that. And she doesn't need any more toys."

Jim looked hurt. "She did so tell me. She whispered it. I know the books say kids can't talk yet, but *she* does. She's a little worried about upsetting you, so she doesn't want me to tell you." He lowered his voice conspiratorially. "You need to pretend you don't know."

He looked completely serious, Heather thought, trying not to laugh. As if he believed every silly thing he said. How was she supposed to resist a man with a perfect sense of the ridiculous?

Perfect. There was that word again.

She sighed. "Fine. We can go through the toy department, but you are not allowed to buy her anything."

"Of course not." He looked hurt at even the suggestion.

Heather knew better than to believe that expression. They would get into the middle of the doll aisle and he would go crazy picking out a half-dozen things for Diane. She'd seen it happen before.

There are worse things, she reminded herself. Jim was a lot of fun and he genuinely cared about her and her child. Maybe he was a little too indulgent, but they could both survive that.

They walked to the elevator, then waited to go down to the basement. Heather noticed a couple of women glancing at Jim with a hint of longing in their eyes. That she understood completely. He was too good-looking by far. She still had trouble when he smiled and flashed his dimple. Her thighs quivered just at the thought. He was tall and strong and smart and gentle and... And she'd better watch herself or she'd end up doing something silly, like falling for him.

Five minutes later, Jim stood in front of Diane. He held several dolls in each arm. "Which do you like the best?" he asked.

Diane blinked but otherwise didn't respond.

"You're ignoring me," Jim said patiently. "I'm going to hold these up one by one and you let me know which one you want." He held up the first doll, a cloth beauty with cotton curls, and shook it. Diane yawned.

Heather stood by the stroller. "You shouldn't be doing this. I've already said she has more stuff now than she'll ever play with. She's a baby. Toys aren't that important."

"I know all that, but what you keep forgetting is that I'm not just doing this for her. I'm doing it for me. I like buying her things." He returned his attention to Diane. "Okay, so none of these work. Let me get another batch."

He walked down the aisle, both putting the dolls he already had back in place and collecting new ones. Heather didn't know whether to laugh or strangle him.

"Your husband is very devoted to his daughter," a voice said from behind her.

Heather turned and saw an older woman smiling at her. She held several toys in her arms.

"I couldn't help overhearing your conversation," the woman continued. "You have a very lovely family. That's nice to see."

Rather than trying to explain the situation, Heather said, "Thank you. I feel very lucky."

The older woman waved and walked toward the cashier.

Heather stared after her. No doubt she and Jim did look like a married couple out with their baby on a Saturday afternoon. A wave of sadness and longing swept over her. Part of her wanted it to be true—if not with Jim, then with someone else. There were times when it was difficult to be alone.

But she'd already had her chance. Three chances,

in fact, and each time she'd struck out. Was she really willing to try again? She knew how to be a good single parent because she'd grown up with one. She wasn't afraid of taking care of Diane on her own. Yet sometimes she was lonely and wanted more. Was that person Jim? She looked at the man patiently trying to get her eleven-week-old baby to pick out a doll. How was she supposed to resist him? How could she not? Nothing in her life had allowed her to experience a relationship with a normal, loving guy who wanted the same things she did. Why would she think her luck was about to change now?

Heather heard Jim's tuneless humming as he prepared the barbecue for their steaks. She finished burping her daughter, then set Diane down to sleep.

"I love you, sweet cheeks," she murmured as she stroked her baby's face. Diane made a soft cooing sound, more breath than vowel, but it was enough to make Heather smile. "You're a special little girl, aren't you?"

Heather pulled the drapes shut, then stepped out of the room and into the hallway. She followed the sound of Jim's voice and found him on the patio, carefully lighting the charcoal he'd poured into the barbecue.

"This will take a little time to heat up," he said without turning to look at her. "Give me thirty more seconds and I'll join you inside."

She moved back into the living room. As she did so, she wondered how he'd known she was behind him. She didn't think she'd made any noise, nor was she wearing perfume. He'd just known. The way she sometimes knew things about him.

It was just the result of their spending several evenings together each week, she told herself. They were friends, nothing more. But she couldn't help the warmth that spread through her or the flash of fear that followed. What was that expression? Damned if she did and damned if she didn't.

Two large bags stood by the front door. They were the wedding presents Jim had purchased earlier that day for Rick and Lupe's wedding. Heather had steered him clear of an incredibly ugly, incredibly expensive ceramic clock and had instead persuaded him to buy several items from their gift registry.

She glanced around the room. On the sofa was a big bag containing a stuffed bear several times larger than Diane. Jim had insisted it was exactly what the infant needed, and that as she got older, she could sleep with it and never have to worry about being afraid of monsters in the closet. Heather didn't completely agree with his reasoning, but she'd given up protesting after about ten minutes of heated argument. Some things just weren't worth winning.

Her gaze moved to the new mini blinds in the living-room window. Mini blinds she'd purchased six months before but had never found time to hang. In the kitchen and bathroom she had new towel racks, and her bedroom furniture had been shifted so that the morning sun no longer shone directly into her eyes. All compliments of Jim. He'd also put together most of Diane's furniture and fixed the baby monitor when it had suddenly stopped working.

"You're looking serious about something," Jim

said as he came in the back door. "Everything all right?"

"Yes." She pointed to the sofa, then went into the kitchen to get him a beer. She collected a glass of water for herself. "I was just thinking about everything you've done in the house," she said as she returned and took a seat at the opposite end of the sofa.

He paused in the act of opening the bottle and frowned. "Are you going to get all feminist on me and tell me that you resent a man helping?"

She laughed. "Not at all. I appreciate your help. Most of the stuff I could have done on my own, but I'm willing to admit that it was nice to have assistance."

He didn't look convinced.

"I swear I'm telling the truth," she said, crossing her heart. "I grew up with a mother who learned to do a lot on her own. She was really good at it, but she would've liked having a man to help around the house, especially with anything heavy. I would've put up the mini blinds myself, but by the time they arrived, I was a little too pregnant to feel comfortable standing on a ladder, so they had to wait."

"If you hadn't helped me, I wouldn't have picked out the right present for the wedding," he said cautiously, as if still worried that she might yell at him. "I'm terrible at choosing ties."

She shifted until she was facing him, then tucked her right leg under her. "If you're trying to make me feel that we each contribute the same in the helping category, you're not doing a very good job, but don't worry about it. I was making an observation, not complaining. You've been very kind to me and I appreciate it.''

He eyed her warily, then nodded. "You're welcome."

She chuckled. "I mean it. Maybe if I'd grown up with a father in the picture, I would've expected this sort of behavior from a man, but for me it's a new experience. One that I'm enjoying."

"Okay. I'll relax." He took a drink of beer, then glanced at her. "At the risk of starting trouble again, what happened to your dad?"

"He left when I was born. Stayed with my mother until I popped into the world, then he walked out. She never heard from him again."

Jim frowned. "Ouch. That had to be tough for both of you."

Heather shrugged. "She always told me she knew it was bound to happen. He wasn't the kind of man who could deal well with the responsibility of a family. She said that having a wife had been enough trauma for him." She paused. "I don't know what to think. I never knew the man, so I try not to make any judgments. My mom was disappointed, but she never hated him. I suppose the hardest thing for me to deal with was the rejection."

"What are you talking about?" he asked.

"My father walked out the second I was born," Heather explained. "It's difficult not to take that personally."

"But it wasn't about you—it was about the responsibility of a family. He would have left any child."

"I know you're trying to make me feel better. And

you're not saying anything I haven't already told myself. But it *feels* like it was about me. I was the only child involved."

Jim's blue eyes darkened with empathy. "I'm sorry."

It was a polite phrase, yet coming from him it made her feel a little better. Probably because she knew he meant it.

"Thanks. It was a long time ago. I've gone through stages when I hated him, when I prayed for him to come home. I've thought about trying to find him. My mom always said that she would give me what little information she has if I want to hire a detective or something."

"Did you?"

"No. I never saw the point. The entire time I was growing up he wasn't interested in me, so why should I be interested in him now? If he came looking, I don't think I would be that hard to find, but it has to come from him. I've made peace with my past."

Jim took a long swallow of beer, then set the bottle on the coffee table. He faced front, resting his elbows on his knees and lacing his fingers together. "I wish I could do that," he said grimly.

"What do you mean?"

He gave a quick jerk of his head. "Nothing." Then he glanced at her and smiled faintly. "I don't suppose you're going to believe that, are you?"

"No, but if you really don't want me to push, I won't."

"It's no big deal," he said. "My dad walked out on me, too. I was a little older and I don't think it was about me, but he left all the same."

Heather pressed her lips together to hold back all her questions. There was so much she wanted to know. Yet something inside of her whispered that Jim had to tell the story at his own pace. So she remained quietly in place on the sofa and waited.

"I guess my parents were happy," he said at last. "They fought some and then they made up. I remember things being pretty good between them. When I was about eight, my mom was diagnosed with MS. After that, everything changed."

Heather's breath seemed to freeze in her throat. "Multiple sclerosis?" she asked in a whisper.

He nodded.

Heather didn't know what to say. What could she say? An illness like that put a lot of pressure on a family. Jim had been only eight years old. "You must have been scared."

"I didn't understand what was happening," he admitted. "She wasn't sick like with the flu, but she was having trouble moving around and doing certain things. Hers was the kind that progressed fairly quickly without many remissions. My dad stayed for two years, then, when I was ten, he walked out on us."

"He left you?" she blurted without thinking. "Just like that? While your mom was sick?"

He nodded.

"Were the two of you alone?"

"Yeah. Neither of my folks had much in the way of family. That's when I got so scared. That's what I remember most about that time. My mom had just started using a wheelchair. It was tough for her to get around the house because some of the doorways weren't wide enough. I couldn't carry her or anything. We had decent medical insurance and sometimes there were nurses, but it wasn't enough. My dad sent money, but that wasn't enough, either.''

Heather's stomach tightened as she tried to imagine a grown man leaving his ten-year-old son in charge of a disabled woman.

''When he left, he said it was up to me. That I would have to be in charge and take care of things. I didn't understand what he was saying. When I started to cry, he slapped me across the face and told me to quit acting like a girl.''

Heather pressed her hand to her mouth to hold in a soft cry of pain. Pain for him and the child he had been. She slid toward him on the sofa but didn't touch him. She wasn't sure if she should encourage him to keep going on with his story or tell him to stop. She wanted to do whatever would make him feel better. But before she could decide what to do, he started talking again.

''My mom got progressively worse. I would come home from school every day and take care of her.'' He closed his eyes against memories she couldn't begin to imagine. ''She suffered a lot.''

''So did you,'' she said gently, and touched his arm. ''You were too young to be dealing with that kind of pressure. I'm surprised the court didn't put you in a foster home.''

''I don't think anyone knew. The nurses came during the day and they all thought my dad was at work. My mom didn't tell them anything different. I think she was afraid of going to a nursing home.''

He clutched his hands tighter, until she could see white on the knuckles and the ridges of his tendons.

"I tried," he said. "I tried so damn hard, but it was never enough. The more incapacitated she became, the more I had to do for her. Finally, the nurses told us she was going to have to go on a respirator."

A shudder rippled through him. His voice dropped to a whisper. "That night, my mother told me she didn't want to try anymore. She was in pain and she was dying. She refused to live her last days breathing with the help of a machine. So she wanted to kill herself."

Heather sucked in a breath. She sensed what was coming next and didn't want to hear it. She didn't want to know what Jim had been through. But she couldn't stop him from speaking. She could only listen and pray that she was wrong.

"I was feeding her soup," he said. "She looked at me and told me she couldn't do it herself, so she wanted *me* to kill her."

The scent of the heating coals drifted into the room. Two houses away, children played outside—a noisy game that had them shrieking with laughter. But here in Heather's house, time stood still. The words repeated themselves in her brain, bending and weaving together until the vowels and consonants made no sense. And yet a very clear image remained. A dying mother had asked her young son to kill her.

"How old were you?"

"Thirteen." He sagged back against the sofa and rubbed his face. "I couldn't do it. I cried and yelled at her and told her it was wrong, but she was relentless. Day after day that was all she talked about.

She'd figured out how and she even wanted me to help her write a letter so everyone would understand it wasn't my fault. She said if I didn't do this one thing, she would never forgive me. She would stop loving me.''

The last sentence had been a mere whisper. Heather had sensed it more than heard it. She stared at Jim, numb with shock, but he wasn't looking at her anymore. She doubted that he even remembered she was in the room.

''The day they came and put the breathing tube into her, she screamed at me, swearing she would never forgive me. Then she stopped screaming. After that, she wouldn't look at me except with hatred.''

Heather's stomach lurched uneasily while cold sweat dotted her brow. It wasn't supposed to be like this for anyone, she thought in horror. How had he survived the ordeal? How had he turned out so incredibly wonderful when this was his past?

''After that, she deteriorated fairly quickly,'' he went on.

His voice had changed, now sounding almost normal, as if he was telling someone else's story. Maybe that was how he kept his sanity.

''They moved her to a nursing home. By that time, I was in foster care. I visited her every day, but when I came into the room, she closed her eyes. No matter how I begged her to forgive me, she pretended I wasn't there. Even at the end, she wouldn't forgive me. I remember standing by the side of her bed, sobbing. I told her that I'd done the best I could, but I couldn't fix her. She was my mother, so I couldn't kill her. I could only love her and want her to love

me back. I begged her to give me just one look to let
me know it was okay between us.''

He was silent for several minutes, then he continued. ''Finally, I bent over to kiss her goodbye. The
doctor told me she probably wouldn't make it through
the night and I begged her one last time to forgive
me. Instead, she kept her eyes closed, and with what
I guess was her last bit of strength and ability to
move, she turned her head away.''

He gave a half-strangled laugh that was one of pain
rather than humor. ''She could only move about a half
inch or so, but I knew what she was doing. Rejecting
me with that final act. She shut me out forever.''

''I'm so sorry,'' Heather said, wishing she had
something helpful to say. She couldn't remember ever
feeling so incredibly inadequate.

''Me, too,'' Jim said lightly. ''I didn't mean to
make you cry.''

She reached up and was surprised to find her
cheeks damp. She sniffed and wiped away the tears.
''What a horrible experience,'' she said. ''It's so sad.
I don't pretend to understand what your mother was
suffering, but it must have been awful. Even so, I
can't forgive her for what she did to you. You were
so young.'' More tears rolled down her cheeks. She
brushed them away impatiently. ''Sorry, Jim. I don't
think I can help it.''

His jaw tightened. ''I wish I'd been able to fix the
situation, to fix her, but I couldn't. That's what I regret the most.''

He was lying. Heather knew that with the same
certainty that she knew the sun would rise the next
morning. Jim was in pain, not because he hadn't been

able to ''fix'' his mother, but because she'd made an impossible request and then rejected him for failing her. What he remembered most was the withdrawal of her love because that was her real death to him.

Then everything made sense. In one of those blinding flashes of truth, she knew why she hadn't been able to figure him out. Why he appeared so perfect all the time. Jim had decided to spend his life making up for what he saw as the failures of a thirteen-year-old boy. He couldn't fix his mother, but he was determined to fix everything else in his world. He was making up for the past. Unfortunately, until he understood he had done nothing wrong, he was destined to search for a forgiveness that could only come from within himself.

There weren't any dark secrets save the one he'd just shared. He was exactly who he appeared to be—a real, live, genuine hero. He really was one of the good guys, and Lord help her, now there was nothing to keep her from falling helplessly in love with him.

Chapter Nine

"You didn't eat much dinner," Jim said as he collected the plates and carried them into the kitchen.

"It wasn't the cooking, I swear. The steaks were delicious."

Heather wasn't lying. The meat had been perfectly prepared. She'd microwaved potatoes and fixed a salad while Jim had barbecued the steaks. But her lack of appetite wasn't because of a problem with the food and they both knew that.

"I'm sorry," he said when he returned to the table and took the seat across from hers. "I shouldn't have told you."

"No." She shook her head. "I'm glad you did. We're friends and you're very important to me. I'm just having a little trouble absorbing everything you said."

Images and questions swirled in her head. The horror of Jim's past made her want to hold him close and somehow make it better. Which wasn't all that different from his own need to fix. As a new mother who deeply loved her child, Heather couldn't understand how either of Jim's parents could have treated him that way. First his father deserting his son and his stricken wife, then his mother with her impossible request. No one should have to deal with that kind of situation, let alone a young boy.

She could feel tears forming again. She'd have to stop thinking about it so much or she would spend the evening sobbing hysterically. Hardly the relaxing good time they'd both planned.

"Let's change the subject," she said. "It's summer, right? So how are the Dodgers doing?"

Jim gave her a lazy grin. "You really want to talk about baseball?"

"Sure."

"Prove it. Name one Dodger player."

She opened her mouth, then closed it. "I know their uniforms are blue and white. That should count for something."

"It should, but it doesn't. I have a different topic suggestion."

"At this point I'm willing to accept anything."

"How about coming with me to Rick and Lupe's wedding?" He held up his hand. "Not as a date, but as friends. I think it would be fun."

"I'd like that," she said without hesitating.

She *would* enjoy spending time with Jim away from the office. She always had. His clarification that it wasn't a date meant she could relax and not worry about subtle or not-so-subtle tension flaring between them.

"Do you dance?" she asked teasingly.

"I think I can shuffle my way around the floor well enough to keep you happy."

"Yes, but will I be embarrassed?"

He laughed. "Probably."

At the sound of his laughter, tears formed in her eyes. Before she could control them, one slipped down her cheek. Jim swore under his breath, reached across the small table and brushed her skin.

"I'm sorry," she said softly. "I'm really fine."

"Yeah, I can tell."

"No, I mean it. Some of it's because I'm still a little emotional these days, and some of it's because of what you told me. Regardless, I refuse to regret knowing the truth about your past. You've had a lifetime to get used to it, but I've only had an hour. Give me a little time and I'll be fine." His hand lay close to hers. She touched it. "I'm very proud to know you."

He stiffened in his chair, straightening and pulling back. "Don't start anything like that. Don't be proud because I survived a difficult childhood. I can name a dozen people who overcame a lot worse."

"It's not that you survived," she said. "It's that you thrived. Look at what you've done with your life. All the people you help every day."

His expression shifted from uncomfortable to embarrassed. He set his jaw. "I'm not some damned hero. I'm just..." He shook his head and stood up. "It's getting late. I should head out of here."

Heather rose to her feet, as well. "You're just a

good man," she said, completing his sentence. "There aren't enough of those around, which still means you get to be a hero whether you like it or not. Sorry, Jim, you're stuck with a cape and superpowers."

"As long as I don't have to wear red plastic boots."

"You don't." She led the way to the front door, then paused before opening it. "I meant what I said," she told him. "I *am* very proud to know you. I appreciate your willingness to share a difficult piece of your past with me and I'll respect your confidence."

He shoved his hands into his front pockets. "I trust you, Heather. I never expected otherwise."

His words made her glow with pleasure. Which was silly because they were just friends, and friends looked out for and trusted each other. None of this should have been news to either of them. But his expression of trust made her feel good about both of them.

Impulsively, she raised herself up on tiptoe to kiss his cheek. But he was six-three to her five-seven and she couldn't quite reach. "I'm only going to give you a friendly peck on the cheek," she said laughingly. "It's a combination thank-you and I'm-happy-to-be-your-friend gesture. The least you could do is cooperate."

But instead of bending down or making a joke, Jim hesitated. In that second, doubts crashed in on Heather. They *were* just friends and she'd somehow crossed the line. He wasn't comfortable with that kind of affection. The thought of her kissing his cheek was repellent to him and—

"A kiss would be nice," he said, interrupting her emotional self-flagellation.

But she'd already taken an involuntary step away and now they were too far apart. They stared at each other. He shook his head.

"Did we just have a momentary lapse of communication or are we both incredibly inept?" he asked.

"I don't know. Maybe both."

He smiled, and her world righted itself. "Okay, let's start over," he told her. "I'm going to say goodbye, but first you're going to give me a kiss. How's that?"

"Fine." But too much time had passed and she was suddenly nervous. Kiss Jim? What had she been thinking? They didn't kiss. They teased and laughed and occasionally hugged, but never, ever kissed.

"Great."

He reached out and took hold of her upper arms and drew her closer to him. As he lowered his head, she went up on tiptoe. Her plan had been to kiss his cheek, only he didn't turn his head and she had to make a decision really soon because his mouth was right there and did she pull away and reach for his cheek or—

Their mouths touched in a soft contact that spoke volumes more than her friendly peck had been meant to do. Heather froze. The very sensible part of her brain said that they'd kissed, it was over, and she needed to get this man out of her house. But the sensible part of her brain was small and incredibly overrated. Especially as the contact between their mouths continued and various parts of her body woke up and began to notice.

At first there was just the pressure of his lips against hers. The warmth and firmness, the masculine scent of his skin, the way his hands moved up and down her arms from elbow to shoulder. Then a tiny flare of heat drifted slowly from her mouth, down her throat, through her chest, before exploding in her stomach, bathing her whole body in a sensual glow. A shiver rippled through her, all the way to her toes, and she was lost.

She placed her hands on his shoulders and felt the lean strength of him. His hands moved from her arms to her back. She took a step closer, or did he? She wasn't sure, but suddenly, their bodies pressed against each other, and then his head tilted to the side, or was it hers? And then the kiss got a whole lot more interesting.

He parted his mouth and she felt the soft dampness of his tongue brushing against her lower lip. She moaned low in her throat even as she opened to admit him. This was insane, she thought through a fog of wonderful need and desire and electric shocks that set all her senses to tingling. This was amazing.

As his tongue invaded her mouth, she welcomed him. They touched and retreated, then touched again, discovering each other in that glorious dance that is the first real kiss. Around again and again, he stroked against her. She could taste his sweetness and feel his breath against her cheek. It was perfect and magic and she never wanted either of them to stop.

She clutched at him with one hand and with the other stroked the back of his head. His hair was silky smooth and still a little too long. His hands were everywhere, moving up and down her back, then lowering to cup her rear and haul her up against him. She felt the flat planes of his chest, the broadness of him, then the hard ridge of his desire pressing against her.

The proof that he wanted her as much as she was realizing she wanted him made her shiver with delight. Wicked images rose up in her mind—of her pressed against a wall, with him supporting her as he drove into her again and again. Of wild lovemaking on the bed, the floor, in the shower, everywhere. She had the startling realization that no single kiss had ever made her dampen so quickly or so much. She was more than hungry for him—she was starving.

He broke the kiss and breathed her name. She answered with a sigh and another kiss. This time, he welcomed her as she slipped past his lips and explored him. She felt the hardness of his teeth, the rough smoothness of his tongue, and as she plunged inside, she wished he were plunging inside her, but in a very different way.

He stroked her hip, then moved up to her breast. Heather had the fleeting thought that he would find her too bony and thin to be attractive. As she always had, she wished she had the lush curves of those women always trying to lose twenty pounds. Just once in her life, she wanted some part of her body to be excessive. But what he was doing felt too good for her thoughts to stay focused on her fears. He cupped her breast gently, a brief touch she barely registered before he was gone again, stroking her side and her arm.

Her nipples had hardened and pressed against her bra, and she asked for him to touch her there. Then he shifted so that he was kissing her jaw and her neck, and she forgot everything except the warmth in her belly and the weakness in her legs. She wanted to lean against him and have this go on forever. He nibbled on her earlobe and made her squirm against him. She reached down and cupped *his* rear and he groaned, and then it didn't matter about curves or lack thereof. There was only the heat and the need, the frantic pounding of her heart, and if she didn't have more of him right now, she would die.

His hands moved faster and faster, up and down her body. When he bent over and gripped the backs of her thighs, it was as if he'd read her mind. She gave a little hop, then she was up in the air, pressed against the door, and he was pushed hard against her, center to center. Hard and throbbing to wet and swollen. He rubbed back and forth, the layers of clothing adding to the friction.

"I want you," he breathed in her ear.

"Yes," she gasped.

"Now."

She reached for the buttons on his shirt, then paused. "I can't."

Jim slowly lowered her to the floor.

She stared at him. "Did I just say that?" she asked. Her mind was a blank. Had she thought the sentence or really said it? "I didn't mean it. Of course I can do this. I *want* to do this." How could she not want it? She was more aroused than she'd ever been in her life. But...

Jim's breathing was still ragged. Need tightened the lines of his face and his eyes burned with fire. He pushed his hair off his forehead, then sucked in another breath. "You're right," he said slowly. "We can't do this."

"No, I'm *not* right." She told herself to take off her shirt or his shirt or something. But she couldn't seem to move. She squeezed her eyes shut. "I can't believe I'm being sensible. What a horrible time to start a nasty habit."

He gave a strangled laugh. "One of us has to be."

"No, we don't. There's no law that says being sensible is required." She looked at him. "I want you."

He took her hand and placed it on the hard bulge in his jeans, then released her. "I want you, too. But there are too many reasons not to do this."

"I love my job," she said glumly. "You're my boss. That would make this kinda tacky."

"Agreed. There's also the fact that neither of us wants to get involved. I like having you as my friend. Becoming lovers would change everything."

She leaned forward and hugged him. "I'm sorry I started this."

"I'm not, although we'll have a hell of a time pretending it never happened."

She laughed. Her body ached with a desperate kind of need she'd never experienced before. They'd come within seconds of doing it right against her living-room door with her daughter due to wake up at any moment. She wasn't on birth control and doubted Jim had any with him. Despite all that, she could still laugh with him.

"I think I should go," he said. "If I stay here much longer, there's no telling what could happen."

"On the contrary. I think we know exactly what would happen." She was still confused about everything, most especially how they'd gone from friendly to passionate in less than ten seconds.

He kissed the top of her head. "Friends?" he asked.

She stepped back and nodded. "Absolutely. I'll see you on Monday."

"Have a good evening," he said, and was gone.

Heather closed the door behind him and tried to figure out what had just happened. Although she could replay the events in her mind, she wasn't at all sure what they meant. Was she crazy or was Jim? Maybe it had been the emotional conversation before dinner. Oh, well. They were going to have to figure out a way to put this behind them.

She headed for her daughter's room, clicking on lights as she went, then paused in the hallway. For the first time since she'd moved into the apartment, the small space felt too quiet and too empty. As the tingles in her tummy faded, something else took their place. It was only after she'd fed Diane and put her back to bed that she realized the odd, almost hurting knot in her stomach was loneliness. She found herself in the painful position of wanting the one thing she couldn't have.

"I know you think she's attractive," Flo said as she dropped several flight-record books on Jim's desk.

Why did women always do this to men? Jim wondered. Start a conversation with the sole purpose of setting the guy up. "She's cute," he said cautiously.

"Cute? She's more than cute. You think she's a pretty hot number and I want to know what you intend to do about it. You can't sit on your butt forever. In case you were wondering, there isn't another man in her life.'' Flo leaned forward, bracing her arms on his desk. ''Women like her don't come along every day. You're crazy if you let her go.''

''Heather and I are friends, nothing more,'' he said, ignoring the memory of the kiss they'd shared the previous weekend and the swift and rather predictable physical result of those memories. Pray God Flo didn't ask him to stand up right now, or she'd get an eyeful.

''That is so much bull, I'm sorry I'm wearing open-toed shoes.'' Flo glared at him. ''What are you waiting for? She's single, attractive, smart and a great mother. You're devoted to her daughter. Heather hasn't gone into detail, but you don't have to worry about Diane's father showing up any time soon.''

He was startled to realize that he knew more about Heather's personal life than Flo did. She trusted him. He'd always known that she did, but hearing proof gave him a warm feeling in his chest. It matched the heat down below. Neither of which counted for spit.

''I don't do commitment,'' he said firmly. ''I'm not the right man for Heather.''

Flo straightened. She wore a sleeveless shirt tucked into a straight skirt, both yellow. Her summer tan was more freckles than brown skin, and she had a big yellow flower in her red hair. She looked charming and he wanted to tell her. Even so, when her gaze narrowed and she stared down at him, he knew better than to change the subject. Flo wasn't kidding about any of this.

''All right. I've given you your chance. If that's

how you really feel, I know a couple of college professors who would be very pleased to meet someone like Heather.''

Jim kept his face impassive. ''You should set up something,'' he said even though his gut felt like it had been ripped open. He could feel his life's blood seeping away. Heather with another man? How was he supposed to survive that?

He leaned back in his chair and told himself he'd better figure out a way to get through it. It was fine that he didn't want Heather for himself, but that didn't mean she was going to spend the rest of her life alone. Despite her protestations to the contrary, she was certain to find herself attracted to someone. As he'd told her, she was too young and had too much to offer to go through life without a man at her side.

If only it could be different. If only it was safe for him to love her. But he couldn't. He wasn't afraid for himself, but for her. He didn't know how to get relationships right, and if he tried, *she* would end up brokenhearted, not him. Worse, she would figure out he wasn't worth it. How was he supposed to survive that?

It was that damn kiss, he thought glumly. He couldn't get it out of his mind. The feel of her, the taste of her, the way she'd responded to him. Women had wanted him before, but with Heather, he'd felt as if she was on fire. He'd done that to her. He wanted to be with her again and again, learning everything that turned her on, then taking her places neither of them had been. He wanted to spend his life making her weak with desire, satisfying her until she couldn't do anything but cling to him and breathe his name.

"How long are you going to hide?" Flo asked.

Jim blinked. He'd forgotten that she was still in the room. He replayed her question and thought of a couple of glib answers. Then, because he was tired of the pretending, he told her the truth. "Forever."

She sighed. "I suppose the good news is that you're finally admitting you have a problem. Don't they say that's half the battle?"

"It's not a problem, it's a way of life."

"You have to stop this," she said, folding her arms across her chest. "You can't keep on renting people, then turning them loose when they threaten to get too close. It's not right. It's not how we were meant to live. People need to make connections. How can you be so alone all the time?"

Her knowing gaze saw too much, but he'd always known that about her. "This is all I know. It makes me happy, so why can't you leave it alone?"

"For the same reason I won't let you find me another job. Because I care about you, Jim. I'm stubborn and I stick my nose in where it doesn't belong, but only because you're a good friend and I hate to see you like this." She drew in a breath. "I know you care about her even though you never say the words, but some people need more. Some people need to know that they're wanted."

He frowned at her. "What's your point?"

"Are you just going to let Heather walk out of your life?"

He met her gaze without flinching and told her the gut-honest truth. "Yes."

Heather walked over and stood next to Flo, who stood staring out the window. "What are you doing?" she asked.

"Watching Jim change the oil in my car and wondering why he has to be as stubborn as a mule."

Heather followed her friend's gaze and saw Flo's old sedan in the hangar. The front end was up on blocks and long, jean-clad legs stuck out from underneath the vehicle. Just seeing the bottom half of him was enough to get her blood racing and that fluttering starting in the pit of her stomach.

"At least he's better-looking than a mule," she said.

Flo chuckled. "I'll give you that, but the man makes me crazy." She sighed but didn't elaborate.

Heather resisted the urge to pry. In the past couple of days, she'd found herself more interested in her boss than usual. She wanted to know everything about him, especially personal stuff. Obviously, she had it bad.

"He makes everything so difficult," Flo said. "How am I supposed to work with that?"

"Do I know what you're talking about?"

"No. I'm upset because the man won't admit he cares."

"He admits it," Heather said. "He cares about Brian and look how much time he gives him. The kid has only been here a couple of weeks, but already they're great friends."

"I'm not talking about that. I'm talking about male-female relationships. He won't get involved."

"I can't blame him for that," Heather said. "I don't want to get involved, either."

Flo threw up her arms in a gesture of frustration.

"What is it with you two? Why can't you admit what everyone else sees?"

Heather had to force herself to stay relaxed even though her first instinct was to stiffen and run. "What does everyone see?"

"That you two are perfect for each other."

"Ah. Perfect? That's a pretty strong term." She exhaled softly in relief. Flo was speculating about what could be, not about what had happened. Thank goodness no one had guessed about the kiss she and Jim had shared. The kiss that she couldn't stop thinking about.

"Do you mean to tell me that you aren't the least bit interested in a relationship with Jim? That if he wanted to get serious or even married, you would say no?"

"I would say no to marriage," Heather told her. She had been thinking that she might be ready to make love with Jim, but marriage? She wanted to spend the rest of her life avoiding commitments, not running after them. "Jim and I are great friends and that's all either of us wants."

"Fine," Flo said, and turned her back to the window. "I give up. You're both crazy and there's nothing I can do about it. If you want to ignore the obvious, I can't help you. Stay blind, stay stupid and live both your foolish lives alone. See if I care." She stalked off toward the lunchroom.

Heather stared after her. She was sorry she'd upset her friend, but she couldn't lie just to make Flo happy. In truth, she didn't want marriage with anyone, not even Jim. But she would admit to certain feelings. She wanted him in a way she'd never wanted any other man. She would like to find out where that wanting would lead and she didn't necessarily mean only to bed. She wondered how that emotion would grow and change in her life. But with Jim constantly holding her at arm's length, she wasn't going to get much of a chance to find out.

Chapter Ten

The hall was crowded and filled with music and laughter. Jim held Diane in her carrier in one hand and placed the other against the small of Heather's back.

"I'm sure our table is over there," Heather said, pointing to the far side of the room.

"Are you two looking for us?" a familiar voice called.

He and Heather both turned in that direction and saw Flo, Brian and several other employees, along with their dates, seated at a large round table.

Heather looked at him and grinned. "Or our table could be a lot closer," she said, not looking the least big chagrined by her mistake. "Did I ever mention I had trouble reading maps?"

"You don't have to mention it," he said as they

approached their friends. "It's obvious. I'll have to remember not to let you navigate on a road trip."

"We might not get where we're going, but we'd have a really interesting time getting wherever we end up."

Her laugh was unrepentant and he couldn't help grinning in return. He hadn't thought he would enjoy attending Rick and Lupe's wedding, but so far the day had turned out well. While the formal Catholic wedding mass had lasted a long time, he'd found himself caught up in the ritual and the beautiful ceremony. Even Diane, who'd been awake, had stayed quiet, cooing softly during the prayers. There was something strange about being in church with a woman, Jim thought as he settled Heather in her chair, then took the last empty seat which just happened to be next to hers. It made a man think about long-term commitments and what he wanted in his life. Not that he was thinking about getting involved with Heather, or any other woman, for that matter.

"About time you two made it," Flo said, leaning forward and speaking loudly to be heard over the music and talking around them. "Did you get lost?"

"No, I had to feed the baby."

Flo raised her eyebrows. "I'll bet that was real interesting."

Heather shook her head. "You are bad. I used the ladies' room at the church. Jim waited until I was finished, then we came here."

"Okay. So is this like a date?"

At her question, the table went quiet. Jim glanced around and saw all his employees staring at him. "Heather and I are friends," he said. "I asked her to join me as my friend. Anything else you'd like to know?"

"As a matter of fact, yes," Flo began.

Jim shot her a look and she pressed her lips tightly together.

Heather unbuckled Diane and lifted her out of her carrier, then held her in her arms. "Wow, tough crowd," she teased as she smiled at him. "I didn't realize I was risking my reputation by coming here with you."

"I think you're safe."

She winked. "Maybe not. Maybe someone will lock us in a closet together to see what happens."

"Not unless they lock Diane in with us. Your daughter's on a pretty regular feeding schedule."

"I suppose you're right. Saved by the baby."

Then Flo said something and Heather was distracted. Jim listened to the conversation around him but didn't join in. He had too much on his mind.

While he wasn't angry about Flo's well-meant comments, he could have done without them. He didn't want his employees matchmaking. For one thing, he and Heather had come to terms with their relationship and neither of them wanted to change things. For another, he was having enough trouble forgetting their passionate kiss the previous weekend without being reminded of it at every turn. Not that anyone knew about the kiss, but talk of men and women and the things they could do in private together brought the kiss to mind and left him in a very uncomfortable physical state.

He glanced around the large hall Rick's family had rented for the wedding. Streamers, balloons and big white paper bells hung from the ceiling. Round tables had been covered with white tablecloths and decorated with floral centerpieces set on small mirrors. The fine crystal reflected the overhead lights. To the far right was a dance floor, to the left, the low platform where the wedding party would sit and dine.

Heather laughed, drawing his attention back to her. She was wearing a pretty pink dress that shimmered and swayed with her every movement. She'd pulled the sides of her hair up and held it in place with fancy combs. Pearl earrings and a matching necklace hung around her neck. She looked fresh and lovely. To his mind, she was the most beautiful woman in the room.

Flo turned her attention back to Arnie, her longtime boyfriend, and Heather looked at Jim. She smiled. "What do you think?"

"They've done a great job with everything. I'm sure it took a lot of work."

She looked at all the people still milling around. "This represents my childhood fantasy."

"A big wedding?"

"No. A big family. I always wanted lots of brothers and sisters." She smiled ruefully. "I think I missed them as much or more than I missed having a father. Not that I told my mother that. She would have been heartbroken."

"I didn't have a big family, either," he said, but wasn't sure he'd missed it. At times, he'd wished there was someone else to help out with his mother, but mostly he'd prayed that she would be healed.

"I wonder if Diane will feel the same disappointment," Heather said, staring down at her baby daughter. "Sorry, little one, but a big family isn't in the cards for you, either."

"You shouldn't say that," Jim told her. "You don't know what's going to happen. You could still meet someone and want to have a family with him." He made the statement sincerely, ignoring the stab of pain at the thought of her with another man. Living with him, making love with him, marrying him.

"I'm reasonably confident that I—"

The sound of fanfare cut her off. Everyone turned and looked toward the large double doors at the front of the hall. They opened and Rick and Lupe swept inside.

"She's so beautiful," Heather breathed. "And he's so handsome. This is great."

Jim nodded in agreement. Lupe wore a traditional white gown covered in lace and tiny beads. A train trailed after her while a frothy veil tumbled down her back. Rick looked tall and sure in a gray tuxedo. The young couple walked toward the platform. As they reached their chairs, Rick leaned over and kissed his bride. Lupe blushed and the crowd cheered.

"Did you have a big wedding?" Jim asked over the calls of the crowd for another kiss.

Heather shook her head. "We eloped, mostly because there wasn't any money for a wedding." A wistful look crept into her green eyes. "Something like this would have been nice."

"Mr. Dyer, I want to thank you." Jim looked up and saw a plump middle-aged woman sniffing into a tissue. "I'm Rick's mother, Sonia, and I've wanted to speak to you for a long time." More tears flowed.

She waved her hand. "Oh, this wedding. I knew I
was going to cry."

He rose to his feet and awkwardly patted her shoulder. Dark eyes continued to fill.

"Thank you for sharing this day with us, with Rick
and Lupe. But more than that, thank you for all that
you did for my son. For so long I was afraid of the
path he'd chosen. We all tried to get through to him,
but he was a boy who thought he was a man. He
didn't want to listen. But you…" She waved her arms
in the air, then pulled Jim into a bear hug. "There
are no words. So I thank you from the bottom of my
mother's heart."

She kissed him firmly on the mouth, a fairly sur-
prising thing considering she was all of five feet and
he didn't remember bending down to help, and then
she was gone.

Jim swallowed uncomfortably, then dropped back
into his seat. Fearing the worst, he glanced around the
table and saw that every one of his employees had
witnessed the emotional scene. Flo was wiping away
a few tears of her own and Brian's redheaded girlfriend looked awestruck.

"Great," he muttered under his breath.

"Maybe you'd better wear those red plastic boots
after all," Heather said in a low voice.

"They'll look a little funny with the suit."

She grinned and put her hand on his forearm. "It
could be worse," she told him. "His whole family
could be lining up to thank you."

Apparently, Heather was also a prophet, he thought
thirty minutes later as the line in front of him dwin-
dled to a few cousins and an older woman who had

no clue who he was but had thought this was the line for the buffet. Practically every relative Rick had ever known was familiar with the story of how Jim had helped one of their own, and each person wanted to thank him individually.

The band started a new song, something slow and romantic. "Enough of this foolishness," Flo said as she rose to her feet and came around the table. "Give me that darling baby of yours and go dance with our boss."

Jim glanced over at Heather, who shrugged. "I have my orders," she said, getting up and holding out her hand. "Want to dance?"

"Absolutely."

They walked out to the dance floor and joined the other couples already there. Rick had Lupe in his arms. When he saw Jim, he gave him a thumbs-up gesture of approval.

"When all this is over," Jim growled, "I'm having a talk with that young man and explaining that there are some things he needs to keep to himself."

"Afraid everyone will figure out the truth?" She slipped into his arms. "You *are* an amazing guy. You can run, but you can't hide."

"I don't feel very amazing," he said, although *she* did. Heather fitted perfectly in his arms. Knowing the crowd around them would help keep his desire under check, he pulled her close until they were touching from shoulder to thigh. He inhaled the scent of her perfume. "You smell good."

"Thanks. So do you."

He tucked their linked hands close to his shoulder and wrapped his free arm more firmly around her waist. "Did I tell you how beautiful you are today?" he asked.

"About five times, and I appreciate every compliment more than you can imagine."

"Why? Don't you know you're an incredibly beautiful woman?"

She looked up at him. Her eyes were wide and color stained her cheeks. "Wow. No one has ever said that to me before. Thank you. I feel very special."

She was special. So special that the thought of always being like this wasn't the least bit scary. Unrealistic, but not scary. If he were willing to give a relationship and love a try, Heather might be the one woman he would want to be with. Of course, because of how much he admired and respected her, he would never inflict himself upon her. Talk about a no-win situation.

They danced twice more. As they returned to their table at last, a gray-haired older woman stopped them. A boy of nine or ten was at her side. The woman spoke in rapid Spanish.

"She says to tell you that she is Lupe's grandmother," the boy said, then paused to listen. "She says that you were very kind to Rick and that she's glad God has blessed you with a wife and family of your own. Your daughter is beautiful."

Jim shifted uncomfortably, not knowing what to say. "Tell her..." He paused.

Heather smiled at the grandmother and touched her arm. "Tell her that we appreciate her kind words and that we wish Lupe and Rick all the happiness in the world."

The older woman beamed in response, then moved

off. Jim tugged at his collar. "Sorry about that. I didn't know what to say."

"I know." She looked at him with wide-eyed innocence. "Gee, have you noticed we've been getting some not-so-subtle messages from the world at large? An awful lot of people assume we're married. I wonder what that means?"

He closed his hand over the back of her neck. "Yeah, like you want to get married any more than I do."

"Less," she said firmly as she led the way back to their table. "I want to get married even less than you do."

Fifteen minutes later, she was dancing with one of Rick's uncles. Jim watched, trying not to feel annoyed at the way the other man was holding her close. He felt someone move next to him, glanced over and saw Flo.

"Don't you want this for yourself?" she asked.

"Are you referring to the cake on my plate? Help yourself."

She swatted his arm, then motioned to the bride and groom sitting alone at the head table. They stared into each other's eyes and spoke as if the rest of the world didn't exist.

"Marriage," she said. "A family. Heather."

He didn't answer; he didn't have to. Flo knew his thoughts on the subject.

She glared at him. "Women like her don't come along every day."

"You've told me this before. I know you're right."

"How long do you intend to be stubborn and stupid? When are you going to take a chance on love?"

He stared at her earnest expression and the concern darkening her brown eyes. "Thanks, Flo."

"What you really mean is never, right?"

He didn't even have to think before nodding.

"I can't do this," Jim said frantically as he paced from one end of the waiting room to the other.

Heather rolled her eyes. "I knew it was a mistake to bring you. Calm down. This is a well-baby visit. Diane's going to get weighed and measured and the pediatrician will make sure everything is okay with her. Nothing else."

"But he's giving her a *shot*," he said in the same tone of voice reserved for discussing serial murderers. "She'll cry. It will be horrible."

"She probably will cry," Heather agreed. "And guess what? We'll all survive it. Well, except possibly you."

Heather glanced down at her daughter who was perfectly content to play with her bright plastic set of baby keys, then at the other woman sitting in the waiting room. She had a one-month-old in a carrier.

The woman met her gaze and smiled. "It's nice that your husband was able to take time off work to come with you and your daughter."

Heather had given up ever trying to explain her relationship with Jim. "I agree. Although if I'd known what he was going to be like, I would've left him behind."

He glared at her, then slumped into the seat next to her. "Fine. Kick me when I'm down. Can I help the fact that I'm worried about Diane? Is that so horrible?'' He leaned his head against the wall and closed his eyes. "I'm going to be sick," he announced.

The other women giggled softly and Heather had to bite back a smile. The real humor of the situation was that Jim wasn't kidding. While he'd been perfectly calm and capable during her emergency delivery in the elevator, when faced with a well-baby visit that involved getting Diane vaccinated, he fell apart.

Still, she had to admit she was happy to have him along. Even with his melodrama, he was company and another pair of ears to listen to the doctor's instructions. Sometimes she got so caught up in remembering all her questions that she had trouble remembering the answers.

They were a good team. Everyone around them assumed they were married—from Rick's grandmother at the wedding the previous month to the young mother in the waiting room here in the pediatrician's office. She'd teased Jim that it was a sign from God, but now she wasn't so sure it was a joke.

She drew in a deep breath and reminded herself that she'd tried the relationship thing three times in the past ten years and ended up hurt in a big way every time. Jim was a wonderful man even though he had a few issues from his past. She liked him and got along with him and they had a chemistry that she'd never experienced before, but they weren't going to have a romantic relationship together. They couldn't.

At first she'd resisted because of her three-strikes rule. But now she wasn't willing to take the chance and risk losing the friendship she'd come to count on. Jim had become a part of her life and she didn't want him to leave. As long as they were friends, she was reasonably confident that he would be there for her. But if they stirred sex and love into the mix, there was no telling what might happen. Better for both of them to keep the status quo.

"Feeling better?" Heather asked later that evening as Jim drank a beer.

"I told you, I'm fine."

"No way. I thought you were about to pass out when you saw the needle. You screamed louder than Diane."

Jim looked insulted. "I did not scream. I exhaled loudly."

Heather laughed. "You made a shrieky noise that could wake the dead. Poor Dr. Miller nearly jumped out of his skin."

"I don't know what you're talking about," he grumbled, but she could see the faint red tingeing his cheeks.

Heather couldn't resist leaning over and patting his arm. "It's okay. Your secret is safe with me. I'll never let on that you can't handle watching Diane get vaccinated."

"It wasn't that," he said. "It was…" He paused.

"Yes?"

"Something else. I don't remember."

"Oh. Of course. Something else made you cry out like a woman."

Blue eyes turned icy and she half expected to see frost forming in the corners of her living room. "What was that?" he asked.

Heather knew she'd crossed the line. Jim might be a great guy, but he wasn't above a tickling attack that would leave her gasping and crying *uncle*. She cleared her throat. "I didn't say anything. Really." She batted her eyes for effect.

"I thought so."

He shifted so that he was facing her. They sat on the sofa in her living room. Dinner was long over and the dishwasher had nearly completed its cycle.

"Thanks for letting me stay," he said. "I enjoyed watching Diane taste her first solid food."

Heather thought about the mess and the tiny amount her daughter had actually swallowed. "I don't think it was a complete failure, but I don't know that we can call it a roaring success, either. I'll do what the doctor suggested and try it every couple of days until she gets the idea. I guess I should go look at high chairs this weekend."

For her first sampling of baby cereal, Diane had been propped up in Heather's lap. But that wouldn't work for very long.

"You want company?" he asked. "My car has a bigger trunk."

"We'd both like that." She looked at his familiar, handsome face. "You're very good to us."

"Yeah, well." Jim cleared his throat. "Actually, I want to talk to you about that."

"The high chair?"

"No. That you don't seem to mind me hanging around with you and Diane."

"I don't. We have fun." She paused. What was he trying to tell her?

He set the bottle of beer on the coffee table. "I want you to know that I really appreciate the way you let me be a part of your life. I enjoy visiting and spending time with both of you.''

Soft warm fuzzies fluttered inside Heather's stomach. She wasn't sure what Jim was trying to say, but she liked it. Was he going to admit to having feelings for her? Feelings that went beyond friendship? She clenched her hands together in anticipation. Did he want to kiss her again, or maybe do something more intimate? Oddly enough, the thought didn't terrify her, which made the whole thing incredibly confusing. Just this morning at the doctor's office, she'd lectured herself on the importance of maintaining their friendship. Was she willing to risk that if he wanted to?

''But I'm a little concerned about taking up too much of your time,'' he continued.

''Huh?'' Wait a minute. That line of dialogue was not part of her fantasy.

''I don't want to get in the way of your having a life. I'm here several times a week. That doesn't leave you much opportunity for socializing.''

Heather sighed once and released the very short-lived dream that he was changing the terms of their relationship. She was surprised to find herself battling disappointment. How strange.

''Jim, you *are* my social life.''

''I know, and I think you should change that. You need to be dating.''

My oh my, the man was obviously incredibly hot for her body. He couldn't wait to see her going out with other men. Damn. Heather leaned back against the sofa and told herself this was all for the best. She could get by without a lover, but friends were essential. Even as she told herself to be sensible, she couldn't help feeling sad that they weren't going to kiss again.

"What about you?" she said. "At least I've tried to make a relationship work in the past. You've never been married." She turned to look at him. "Why is that? You're perfect husband and father material."

"No way. I'm good at fixing things, but bad with people. I don't do the emotional stuff well."

"Way! You're terrific with people. Look at Rick. His entire family wants to sponsor a shrine in your honor. There's Flo and Brian and practically every other employee at the company. Jeez, Brian is like a little puppy following you around, wanting to be just like you."

"That's a mistake," he grumbled. "I'll admit I like helping people out in their lives, but only with logistical things like jobs or finding an apartment. I don't know how to connect emotionally."

"We're friends. You adore my daughter."

He smiled. A warm, slow smile that made her thighs quiver. "That I do."

"So what's the problem?"

"I'm not what you think."

Heather sat up and glared at him. "That argument is getting really old. The bottom line is you better get ready for a real relationship because one day you're bound to fall in love and have some kids of your own. Don't even try to tell me differently because you have daddy written all over you. I know you want that, so why are you resisting so hard?"

He didn't look at her, but he didn't have to for her to realize that she'd trodden on dangerous territory.

There were other clues. The tension in his body, the tight muscle in his jaw, the steely set of his gaze.

Heather wondered if she should call it all back. Did she really want to know any more of Jim's secrets?

"I wanted that once," he said before she could decide. "I've been in love. In high school. My senior year. Carrie was smart and pretty and I was head over heels for her. Then one day she turned up pregnant."

Heather's breath caught in her throat. Her first instinct had been to be jealous of this Carrie person, but now she could only focus on the fact that Jim had a child. "What happened?" she asked.

He shrugged. "I had a football scholarship out of state, but I told her I would give it all up to be with her. I wanted to make it right. I wanted us to get married." He glanced at her. "Pretty stupid, huh?"

"No. Pretty wonderful." That was so like him, she thought. Her first husband hadn't lifted a hand to do anything to support them, and Luke had walked out on her. But Jim wasn't like that. He would be willing to go the distance.

"I went out and found a job and we looked for an apartment. We couldn't afford much, of course, but I knew everything would be okay. Then one day she didn't come to school. When I called her house, her mom told me she had the flu."

His voice was flat and emotionless. Heather stiffened in anticipation of something horrible. She sent up a prayer that she was wrong, that someone else hadn't destroyed Jim the way his mother and father had. After all he'd been through, he didn't deserve that. But her prayers were years too late.

"Two days later, she came to see me. She told me

she thought we were too young to get married. She wasn't even sure she wanted to marry me, but she was sure she didn't want a child. My child. She'd gone off and had an abortion without even telling me."

Chapter Eleven

Heather didn't think it was possible for Jim to shock her again. Not this much or this way. He was speaking. She could see his lips moving, but she couldn't *hear* him. Not clearly anyway. There was only the rushing sound of her stunned amazement and the burning in her eyes and throat from unshed tears.

"How could she?" she murmured, more to herself than him.

Jim stopped talking and stared at her. "Are you all right?"

"Of course. I'm fine. It's just..." Her voice trailed off. Waves of pain washed over her. Pain for the young girl who had to make such a difficult decision, but mostly pain for Jim. For the young man he'd once been and the man he'd grown into. She shifted on the sofa, moving toward him until she was close enough to rest her hand on his forearm. "I'm glad you told me. That experience explains a lot."

His gaze narrowed. "Like what?"

"Like why it's difficult for you to trust in relationships or love. You must have felt betrayed."

"I did," he admitted. "I'd been willing to go the distance, but she hadn't wanted that." He shrugged. "I guess we *were* too young."

"Did you ever talk about it? Later, I mean?"

"Do you mean did we talk about why she had an abortion without discussing it with me?"

She nodded.

"Yeah."

Jim stared past her. Heather knew he was caught up in the memories of his past. She wanted to pull him close to her and hold him until the ache went away, but she didn't think he would welcome her comfort.

"She said that she knew I would try to talk her out of it."

"Was she right?"

"Probably. I thought we could make it, but she felt the odds were too stacked against us. She wasn't sure she wanted to get married and she knew she wasn't ready to be a mother."

"Do you understand her reasoning?"

He was quiet for a long time. "I've heard all the arguments—that it's her body and ultimately she's the one responsible for the child. I know her family didn't want her to have the baby. But—"

"But it was your child, too," she said gently. "You wanted to have a say in the decision."

His troubled gaze met hers. "I would've given up

everything for the two of them. I would've worked two or *three* jobs. I know we could have been okay.''

But the young woman in question hadn't given him a chance to prove himself...or fix the situation. First his mother had asked him to do something impossible, then his first love had taken away his chance to take care of her and their child. No wonder Jim went through life trying to fix things for everyone.

A sudden rage burned through her. She rose to her feet and paced to the window. ''Damn,'' she said aloud. ''I'd like to get my hands on both of them.''

''Both of who?''

''Your mother and that girl. I want to tell them exactly what I think of them!'' Talk about horrible, selfish, thoughtless creatures.

Jim looked startled. ''What are *you* so mad about?''

She turned on him and planted her hands on her hips. ''I'm not mad, I'm *furious.* How dare they do that to you? How dare they treat you so horribly. Your mother had no right to ask you to do what she did. You were only a boy. I sympathize with her pain, but no matter what, she was still your mother and she should never have put you in that situation. As for your girlfriend, you should have had a choice. If she didn't want to get married, fine. If she didn't want the baby, fine. But if you were willing to take the child and be completely responsible, you should have had that option.'' She ground her teeth together. ''I want to do something, but I can't. It's terrible.''

''You're spending a lot of energy on this,'' he said. ''It's old news.''

She looked at him and saw that he believed what he said. He didn't even realize how his past continued to haunt him and influence his actions. She returned to the sofa and sank next to him, then took his hands in hers. "You are such a wonderful man. You deserved better than that."

"What about you?" he asked. "Sounds to me like the men in your life haven't been all that terrific."

He did have a point. "Okay, I'll agree I've had a run of bad luck, but that's changing. After all, now I have you."

Heather stared at him, not quite sure she'd actually said those words aloud. Had she? Had she really said that she had Jim in her life? That was what she meant, but not in the way he was likely to interpret her comment. She jerked her hands free of his, then scooted back to the far end of the sofa.

"What I mean," she began awkwardly, "is that we're friends. I didn't mean that in a romantic way. I meant I have you in my life as a friend and it's a very nice change from the losers I've…" She bit her lower lip. "That didn't sound much better, did it? Okay, let's try this again. What I was trying to say was—"

He cut her off with a brief shake of his head. "I understand your point, but I also want to make sure you understand mine." His gaze lingered on her face. "If I decided to change my rule, I would do it for you in a heartbeat. But I'm not. I don't do relationships, Heather."

"I know," she muttered, wishing the earth would open up and swallow her. This was too humiliating for words. "I'm fine with that. I don't want a relationship, either." Although she wouldn't mind one or two of his fabulous kisses. For a man who didn't date much, he sure was a good kisser. Why was that?

She looked at him, at the piercing blue eyes and the dimple he could flash on command. At the broad shoulders and well-muscled arms. The man filled out a pair of jeans in a way that, in some countries, would be considered illegal. He had to have women falling all over him. When they did, would he give in?

"I have a question," she suddenly announced. Courage momentarily failed her, but then she concluded that she'd already humiliated herself once that evening. It wasn't likely to get a whole lot worse. "What do you do about…well…you know."

"Know what?" he asked, then grinned. "Are you asking about my sex life?"

"I believe I am. You're a normal guy. You have needs and hormones and all that. How do you take care of those needs?"

Jim didn't know whether to be shocked or flattered by Heather's question. He also hoped she didn't notice how big his "need" was right now. He often had trouble controlling his urges when he was around her, but when they were also talking about making love… He shook his head. That made the wanting damn near impossible to keep in check. If only she weren't so pretty or fun to be with. If only she didn't smell so good, or walk with that little sway to her hips, or do any of a dozen other things that made him crazy about her.

But, as he'd already informed her, he didn't do relationships, and Heather wasn't the casual-sex kind of woman. So he would continue to suffer through the pain of unfulfilled arousal as he'd been doing for the past three months. None of which answered Heather's question. Based on her expectant expression, she wasn't going to let him get away without answering.

"I have female friends," he said cautiously.

"Women you see for sex?"

"They're not hookers. I occasionally establish a short-term relationship based on physical needs. Both parties understand that and abide by those rules."

She tilted her head. "An affair."

"Exactly."

Her expression turned thoughtful. "Where do you find them?"

"I meet them through work connections or friends."

"Employees?"

"No."

"Why?"

He thought about that one for a second. "It's never been an issue. Most of my employees are guys."

"Oh. That would sort of change things." She tucked a strand of hair behind her ear. "So you meet a woman, and if you like her, you discuss the possibility of a month or so of exclusive sex. No commitment, no strings."

He didn't like where the conversation had gone. "Yes."

Then he got it. Her questions, her quiet consideration. Horror and anticipation slammed into him, sending him slumping against the sofa. Dear God, she could not possibly suggest what he dreaded she was going to suggest. There was no way he could...they could...it would never work.

Or it would work too well, a little voice in his head whispered. If he were honest with himself, that was his greatest fear. That being with Heather would be all things wonderful. She already knew too much. She was too close, too far inside him. If he wasn't careful, he would start to want her in an emotional way. Then they would be more than friends and he would be lost.

He rose to his feet, crossed to her side of the sofa, bent down and kissed her cheek. "I've got to be on my way."

Her gaze was scornful. "Coward."

"Sensible," he corrected. "One of us has to be."

"It could work."

An affair? With Heather? Never. Because at the end of the appointed time, he wouldn't be able to let her go. He would fall for her, and when she found out the truth about him and left him, he would die.

Heather stood on a chair and tried to reach one of the balloons dangling above her. Some of the ribbons were too short and she couldn't reach them without help. But even if she stood on a chair, the curling yellow ribbons were tantalizingly out of reach.

"I'll do that," a male voice said.

Heather turned around and saw Brian standing in the entrance to the walled-off portion of the hangar. She smiled at the teenager and climbed down. "Thanks. You're a good three or four inches taller, so it should be easy for you."

He jumped up and grabbed the ribbon in one graceful, athletic movement, then handed her the balloon. "Jim asked me to help you clean up."

She glanced around at the half-eaten cake, the melting ice cream and the paper plates and plastic forks that hadn't quite made it into the trash can. "Thank you, sir. I do believe I'll accept your assistance."

Brian flushed slightly, gave her a shy smile, then started clearing the tables.

"Do you want to take the cake home?" Heather asked. The chocolate-frosted gooey confection had marked the celebration of two more employees going on to bigger and better jobs. "We ordered a half sheet this time and about a third of it is left over. I think it would freeze well if your mom wants to do that."

"Thanks," Brian said. "That would be great."

Heather found some plastic wrap in the cabinets on the far wall and wrapped up the cake. As she did so, she kept glancing at Brian. Although she didn't spend much time with him, when she did, he always had a dozen things to talk about. His job, how great Jim was, his girlfriend, school, his career plans, college. But today he was strangely silent. The only sound in the hangar was the rustle of his broom on the cement floor.

Heather gave up all pretense of working and studied him. He looked as tired as she felt. Diane had been up the past few nights. The pediatrician and her mother had both said it was a precursor to teething and there was little Heather could do but try to make her daughter comfortable. She wondered what was keeping Brian up at night.

"Is there something on your mind?" she finally asked.

Brian glanced up, stared at her for a second, then shook his head. "I'm fine."

"Uh-huh." Like she believed that. Maybe if she started a conversation, he would feel more comfortable joining in. She tried to figure out the most helpful opening. He talked to Flo about his girlfriend, so it probably wasn't that. He talked to Jim about nearly everything else.

She paused in the act of closing an ice-cream carton. Was that it? Was there a problem with Jim? There was only one way to find out.

"These parties are great," she said. "I like the chance to say goodbye to people who are leaving."

She waited, but Brian didn't do more than nod.

"Jim really takes the time to find his people a job where they'll be happy. Not many employers would bother. Of course, he won't have to do that for you, right? You'll be heading off to college in a year."

"I guess."

She leaned against one of the tables while Brian started stacking the metal folding chairs into neat piles. "Have you talked to him about that?" she asked. "Depending on where you decide to go to college, I'll bet he could help you find a job there working with helicopters. If you want to, I mean."

Brian froze, then shuddered. "He doesn't know me," he said quietly. "I'm just the new guy and a kid. Nobody knows me."

Heather didn't know what that meant, but it gave her a bad feeling. "Brian, what's wrong?"

He brushed his dark brown hair off his forehead and shrugged. "Nothing. I swear." His gaze was intense. "I'd never do anything wrong. I need Jim to trust me on that."

"Well, you've never given him reason not to trust you."

Brian didn't respond. Then he finished stacking the chairs and left without even saying goodbye. Heather was still staring after him when Jim walked into the hangar.

"What's the problem?" he asked.

"I don't know. I just had the strangest conversation with Brian. I think something's bothering him, but he doesn't want to talk about it." She gave him a brief recap of their conversation.

"I don't understand what he was trying to say," Jim told her. "Brian's work around here is helpful, but he doesn't do anything strictly essential. He's not allowed to work on the equipment, so he can't make a mistake there. Why wouldn't I trust him?"

"My point exactly."

"Maybe he just has a lot on his mind."

"Maybe." But Heather wasn't convinced. She decided she would try to speak to Brian in the next few days.

"Life is complicated at seventeen," Jim said.

"I think it's complicated at any age. If nothing else, it's always changing." She picked up the cake Brian had forgotten. "Two more employees leaving. Is that going to be a problem?"

"No, I just hired three more from the college. They start on Monday."

"So you bring them in, train them, then move them on. Don't you ever miss anybody?"

"Sometimes," he said easily.

"But you never think about keeping a few on permanently?"

"No. That's not my style."

His style didn't amuse her, at least not under these circumstances. She couldn't say why it bothered her, but it did. "Sometimes I think you—" The sound of crying cut through the air. Heather looked at the baby monitor she'd brought with her into the hangar and sighed. "She's awake and she's unhappy. I'd better get over to her."

Jim followed her back to the office. "Diane has been fussy these past few days. Is everything all right?"

"Yes. I almost wish there was a problem because then there would be a solution. Unfortunately, all we're dealing with is her teething. She won't actually get teeth for a while, but according to the pediatrician, she's starting to feel some pain. I checked with my mother. She told me that I cried for three weeks straight, although I was fine when the teeth came in later."

Jim held the office door open for her, then walked inside after her. "You look tired."

Heather had tried to cover the dark circles under her eyes with makeup, but obviously she hadn't been successful. "Diane hasn't been sleeping much at all."

"You don't have to come into work if you're not getting any rest."

"Thanks. I'll let you know if it becomes a problem."

A week later, Jim knocked on Heather's door. Even from the front porch he could hear Diane's cries. He waited patiently, then knocked a second time. Finally, he heard the lock turn and Heather peered out.

When she saw him, she gave a weak smile. "Why did I know it had to be you?"

"You haven't been to work in three days. I know you're exhausted and I came by to see if I could help." He held up two grocery bags. "I brought food."

"Talk about a prince among men. Come on in."

He stepped inside. The living room was a little messier than usual, but otherwise it looked fine. He wished he could say the same for Heather. Weariness dulled her eyes. The shadows underneath were darker than he remembered and there were hollows in her cheeks. She wore sweats and a T-shirt, but the shapeless garments couldn't hide the fact that she'd lost weight—something she couldn't afford to do.

"So you haven't been eating, either," he said.

"I know." She walked up and down the length of the living room, holding her crying daughter.

"How long have you been carrying her around?" he asked as he went into the kitchen and began putting the groceries away.

"Days. I mean that literally," she called after him. "I don't think either of us has slept in the past forty-eight hours. Before that, she was crying for three or four hours straight. I figure I've only got another week of this left, but it's hard to get through."

Jim paused in the act of sliding milk into the refrigerator. Had that been a break he'd heard in her voice? He quickly closed the door and returned to the living room.

"I'm trying to be a good mother," she said, her voice suddenly thick with tears. "I want to do the right thing, but I don't know how to make her feel better or help her get some sleep." She sniffed.

Jim couldn't help staring at her. In all the time he'd known Heather, she never complained, never whined and certainly never cried. The only tears he'd seen had been tears of joy after Diane was born. And she was strong. She'd even stayed calm while giving birth in an elevator assisted only by a stranger who didn't know what the hell he was—doing. He liked giving things to her and helping out, but mostly because it made *him* feel better. He never thought of her as being in need.

"You're crying," he said.

She sniffed again, then wiped her cheek with her arm. "No, I'm not. I've been walking so much my eyeballs are sweating. I don't cry. I'm not some weak, mindless female. I'm tough and independent. I'm fine. We're both fine." The volume of Diane's cries went up a notch. Heather moaned. "Someone please tell me what to do."

He didn't have any answers so he did the only thing he could think of. He walked over to her and took the baby. Then, with his free hand, he hugged Heather close. "It's going to be all right," he murmured against her soft, sweet-smelling hair. "You don't have to go through this alone. I'm right here."

"But I don't want to depend on you."

"You're not. You're borrowing me for a short period of time. There's a difference."

"But I can't do that. It's—" She froze in his arms. "Do you hear that?" she whispered.

He listened. "I don't hear anything."

"I know. She's quiet. She must have missed you."

Jim glanced down and saw that Diane had fallen asleep in his arms.

"Don't move," Heather breathed.

"I can't stand here forever."

She looked as if she wanted to argue.

"Tell you what," he said. "I'll put her down. If she wakes up while I'm doing that, I'll take responsibility for getting her quiet again."

He moved slowly into Diane's room and put the sleeping baby into her crib. Diane stirred and snuffled, but she didn't wake up. He straightened and turned, then saw Heather leaning against the door frame.

Light from the living room spilled into the hall and illuminated her from behind. She looked slight and tired, but still beautiful. Even without makeup and in an old T-shirt and sweats. He wanted her at that moment as much as he'd ever wanted her. But he'd grown used to ignoring the desire, so he walked out of the room and closed the door behind them, all without saying a word.

"Go take a shower," he told her, wishing he could be the one doing that instead. Fifteen minutes in icy water just might take away his need for her. At least temporarily. "After that, you can take a nap. I'll watch Diane and walk with her if she wakes up."

Heather closed her eyes and sighed. "A shower. That would be fantastic." She was already heading across the hall to her bedroom. "I'll only be ten minutes."

"Take your time," Jim called, knowing that it wouldn't matter if it was one minute or an hour. The entire situation was torture.

He returned to the living room, turned on the television and started flipping through channels. Nothing caught his attention, so he turned off the machine. As much as he wanted to pretend otherwise, he was stuck, so he might as well give in. He leaned back, closed his eyes and thought about Heather…naked…and dripping wet, then wished he was brave enough, or stupid enough, to join her.

Chapter Twelve

Heather tilted her head back to let the hot water rinse her hair. It was just exhaustion, perhaps physical, mental or both. It was the phase of the moon. It was the fact that no man had the right to look so incredible in a pair of jeans. It was...insane, she decided at last, turning under the spray. She absolutely, positively, could *not* start something with Jim. They were too different. They wanted different things.

She paused and stared blankly at the white tiles in front of her. Actually, she wasn't sure what either of them wanted, but if she did know, they would be different. Besides, they both did want one thing, and that was not to get involved. No relationship, no romantic entanglement, no man-woman thing messing up a perfectly good life. So why was she standing here in her shower thinking about doing the wild thing with the man sitting in her living room?

She turned off the water and slid open the glass door. After grabbing her towel, she started drying herself. It was fine to want him, she told herself. Wanting was acceptable. Everyone had an imagination. The fact that hers had been working overtime lately was interesting news but not life changing. She could fantasize and daydream and wish as long as she didn't *do* anything about it.

She and Jim couldn't become lovers. For one thing, she didn't know if he was interested, although based on their kiss, she thought he might be. For another, they already had a nearly perfect relationship and why would she want to risk ruining that? And there was her three-strikes rule—she should know better than to get involved. He would be way too easy for her to fall for. Although if it was simply about physical intimacy and not about falling in love, then—

"Stop it," Heather said aloud. She toweled her hair, then wrapped the thick cotton around her body, tucked in the corner to keep it in place and moved to the mirror. "I'm not going to do anything about this. I'll get dressed, go out there and have a normal conversation with him. Just the way I have a thousand times before. Nothing is different. We can't do this."

As she stared at her reflection, she saw the wanting in her eyes. She *did* want him, and in her tired, vulnerable state, it would be difficult to keep that knowledge to herself. The truth was she wanted Jim in her bed. Their kiss had been incredible and she wanted to feel that passion again. She'd had three lovers in her life and knew what it was like to be with a man. She understood and had experienced pleasure, but she'd never been on fire before. She wanted to know how it would feel to have those flames everywhere. She wanted Jim's strong hands on her body, touching her, taking her places she'd never been. She trusted him—how could she not? He was a wonderful man.

Heather combed her hair, then quickly dried it with the blow-dryer. After smoothing on tinted moisturizer, she used a little mascara and stepped back. What if it wasn't emotional? she wondered. What if it was just about two friends sharing incredible, sinus-clearing sex? Wasn't their relationship strong enough to handle that? Couldn't they have the best of both worlds—a warm, caring relationship and physical intimacy without all the messy romantic junk? Was she brave enough to try to find out?

In her heart of hearts, she knew Jim would never make a move on her. Which meant she had to be the one to initiate anything. What if he said no? Would she die from the rejection? She drew in a deep breath. The answer to that last question was certainly no. Embarrassment only felt like dying, but nothing really happened. If he said no, well, she would pick herself up and get on with her life. Worse things had happened.

She went into her bedroom and tried to figure out what to put on. Something sexy? Something casual? Panic tightened her stomach. If only she knew if he really wanted her.

She walked to her dresser, pulled open every drawer, then closed them one after the other. "Maybe I'll just arrange myself artfully on the bed," she muttered. "After a couple of hours, he'll get worried and come check on me. If I'm naked, he might get the picture."

Of course, he might take one look at her bony body and run screaming into the night.

Jim threw down the baby magazine. In the past twenty minutes, he'd forgotten how to read. That was the only explanation why the words danced around the page like so much gibberish. He'd already tried pacing, but all that did was bring him way too close to Heather's bedroom door. Which made him think about opening it, stepping inside and joining her in her shower. Which made him break out into a cold sweat. He was hard and ready and tense and he just wanted to get the hell out of here.

What was wrong with him? He'd been in the house with Heather dozens of times. Sure he'd always wanted her, but the needing had been controlled. Something had happened and he couldn't figure out what. Maybe it was the shower, the image of her naked body, slick and—

Her bedroom door opened. Jim bit back a curse. He hoped she didn't ask him to move for the next several minutes because there was no way he could stand up without her getting an eyeful of his aroused state. He would think about something else, something calming and not the least bit sexual. Tractors, or helicopters. That was it. He would mentally review his inventory and try to remember what parts needed reordering. He knew he was out of—

"Jim?"

Steeling himself against the inevitable, he glanced up. And sucked in a breath. If he hadn't been sitting, he would have fallen on his butt for sure.

Heather stood in the doorway to the living room.

She wore a short, white terry-cloth robe. A very short robe that belted at the waist and plunged low enough to expose a generous expanse of cleavage. With a certainty he couldn't explain, he knew she was naked under that robe. Naked except for the sweet scent of her perfume.

His body tightened to the point where he thought he was certain to explode. He couldn't speak, could barely breathe. His hands clenched into fists. He wanted her more desperately than he'd ever wanted any woman in his life.

For one brief, wild moment he thought she might be coming on to him. Hope flared, then winked out as quickly. Heather would never do that. Not that he wouldn't want her to, but she wasn't aggressive and she saw him more as a big brother than as a lover. Didn't she? Weren't they both telling each other that they couldn't get involved? He knew *he* couldn't. But that didn't stop him from wanting her or needing her with a desperation that left him immobilized.

"Did you need something?" he said, his voice thick and hoarse.

Her mouth curved in a smile. "What an interesting choice of words. As a matter of fact, I do need something."

Was there a leak in the shower? A blocked sink? A spider in her bedroom?

Then she started walking toward him. He couldn't have said what was different, but he instantly understood the message. Maybe it was the sway of her hips, or the slight thrust of her chin, or the way she led with her chest. In that second, he knew she wasn't looking for help with a plumbing crisis. She wanted a man. More specifically, she wanted him.

The realization added to his desire until he thought he might choke. He watched her come to a stop in front of him and draw in a breath.

"I've never done anything like this before," she admitted quietly.

Her soft hair fluttered around her face and she tucked a loose strand behind her ear. He noticed that her fingers trembled.

"We're both consenting adults," she continued. "Neither of us is interested in a traditional, romantic relationship. Neither of us wants to get involved. But that kiss was pretty amazing, and I can't help wondering how the rest of it would be. So I thought, if you were interested, we could find out."

Color stained her cheeks, but she held her ground in front of him. He tried to speak, but his throat had tightened to the point where he couldn't even breathe, let alone talk. Images flashed through his brain. Of them together, naked, making love. Just like he'd pictured when she first went into the shower. Only this time he could see those tangled legs and touching bodies and know that it was really going to happen. She wanted him. *She* wanted him.

Heather took a quick step back. "Okay, so I read this all wrong." She ducked her head and turned away. "You probably want to leave now, and I think you should. The earth is not cooperating by opening up and swallowing me, despite my frantic requests that it do so. It would be—"

"No!" he said urgently as her words sank into his brain. He sprang to his feet, moved toward her and spun her to face him. "I want you. Desperately. I'm just having a little trouble thinking that you want me in the same way." His hands tightened on her shoulders as he stared into her eyes. Some of the embarrassment faded from her lovely face. "Tell me you're naked under this," he said.

"As a jaybird."

A shudder rippled through him. He groaned aloud, then pulled her close and pressed his mouth to hers.

As far as kisses went, it was as amazing as Heather remembered. The warm pressure of his lips against hers set every nerve ending in her body to dancing. Heat flared all over, although the most interesting was the damp heat between her legs. Even before his tongue tenderly swept inside her mouth, she could feel the rush of dampness as her body readied itself for his masculine assault.

Her arms came up around his neck. As she stepped closer, he pulled her to him, grabbing her waist, then dropping lower to her rear. She was flush against him, her breasts flattening against his chest, his erection straining against her belly. Their heads tilted and he plunged deeper into her mouth. She stroked his tongue with her own. Over and under and around in ever-changing sensations of rough and smooth, while she savored the familiar, sweet taste of him.

She inhaled the scent of his body, a scent she would know always. There would be no problem finding this man in the dark. She touched his cool silky hair, then moved her hands down his broad back. Muscles tightened in response to her touch. He responded in kind, moving his hands up and down until his palms brushed past the hem of her short robe and touched the bare skin on the backs of her thighs. Instantly, his hardness flexed and they both groaned.

He broke the kiss and stared at her, his blue eyes dark and stormy with a male hunger that made her bones melt. As she watched him watching her, he slipped under her robe and delicately traced the curves of her rear. He moved up the side of her hips, then back and down, cupping and squeezing. His fingertips both tickled and aroused, and she didn't know whether to laugh and duck away or beg for more.

An ache began between her thighs. It pulsed in time with her rapid heartbeat. She wanted to drop to the floor, spread her legs and beg him to take her right there. Then he gripped her rear firmly and raised her. She gave a little hop to help him. He lifted her in the air, pulling her against him as he did. She wrapped her arms around his neck as he carried her toward her bed.

She squeezed her thighs, pressing herself harder against him, wanting him to touch her more intimately. The thick denim, double layered over the fly, kept her from really feeling him, and she had to bite back a cry of disappointment.

"I want you, Jim," she murmured against his ear. She kissed his forehead, his cheek, his jaw. She licked the faint rasp of stubble and bit the edge of his jaw.

He swore, a sharp word that made her giggle.

"Yes, that *is* what we're going to do," she teased.

He paused in front of her bed. "That's not what I meant and you know it," he growled. "I want you, too. More than you'll ever know. But hearing you talk about it and feeling you against me, not to mention the kissing, is making me about ready to explode."

His eyes blazed with fire. "I refuse to embarrass myself like that."

It had never occurred to her that she could bring this strong, incredible man to his knees. Power filled her. Feminine strength and purpose that had her lifting her hips so that she could rub more firmly against him.

He sucked in a breath. Then he was kneeling on the bed. She released her grip and slid down to the mattress. As she did so, her robe fell open. Jim's gaze dropped to her pale breasts, swollen from breast-feeding, then to her narrow rib cage and her stomach, once again flat but now marred by stretch marks.

Heather had to fight not to close her eyes. She knew he would see the jutting hip bones, the skinny legs, the bony shoulders, her small breasts....

He bent over and kissed her, his tongue sweeping inside and brushing against her own. When he withdrew, he trailed kisses down her jaw to her ear. "You're beautiful," he murmured, then nibbled on her earlobe. Tendrils of fire curled through her, all the way down to her toes. "Everything about you is exactly as it should be. I love your delicate slenderness and your smooth, pale skin. Even the marks from your pregnancy are precious. You are perfect in every way, and I want you."

Tears burned at the backs of her eyes. Tears of happiness. For the first time, a man had made her believe he found her naked body acceptable. More than that—desirable. She suspected that Jim was the kind of guy who preferred curves, especially on top, yet he could see past her body to the woman inside. That inner being was the one he was really attracted to, but his passion was such that it spilled over and he thought all of her was beautiful. Why had she ever doubted this man?

"Thank you," she whispered, and pulled him close.

"Not yet." He straightened. "One of us is way overdressed."

While she shrugged out of her robe and tossed it on the floor, he pulled off his boots and socks, then unbuttoned his shirt. Heather rose to her knees.

"I'll help with that."

She moved to the edge of the bed and reached for him. The front of the shirt had parted, exposing a well-muscled chest covered with a light dusting of hair. She placed her hands against his breastbone, then moved them up toward his shoulders. He was strong and his chest hair tickled her palms. She slipped down, sliding over his nipples, pausing to tease the tight points and make him shudder. When she reached his waist, she pulled his shirt free of his jeans. As he let it fall to the floor, she started unfastening his belt. He stopped her.

"I'd better do that," he said.

"Why?"

"If you touch me, it will all be over."

"How very flattering."

So she sat back on her heels and watched him unzip his jeans, then push them and his briefs down. His arousal sprang free—a long, hard shaft that looked smooth and velvety.

They were really doing this, she thought with some surprise. They were going to make love. She paused, wondering if she would have second thoughts. But her brain was quiet and her only sensation was one of rightness. For reasons she didn't understand, she belonged in Jim's arms.

She scooted over on the bed and he lay down next to her. They angled toward each other. He pulled her close so they were touching, just like they had before. Only this time they were both naked, and when her breasts flattened against his chest, she could feel the warmth of his skin and the hair there teasing her nipples. Her slender legs tangled with his. As he kissed her, he drew her left leg over his hip and slipped his right leg between hers.

The tension that had momentarily faded returned again full force. She shifted so that her center pressed against his knee and she rubbed back and forth. The pressure was more frustrating than pleasurable. Her swollen insides wanted stroking and filling and release. She wrapped her arms around him and kissed him back, sending her tongue into his mouth and coaxing him to follow her back. When he did, she bit down gently.

Jim raised his head and stared at her a moment. He looked as startled as she felt.

"I'm sorry," she said quickly. "I've never done anything like that before." She hadn't, either. "I don't know what came over me. I just..."

He smiled at her then, a satisfied male smile that made her squirm in anticipation. She'd awakened the dominant animal that lived in every aroused man. It was a side of him she'd never seen before. For that matter, she'd never seen it in any man.

"Heather?" he asked as if he wanted to make sure this was what she wanted.

"Yes," she said even though she didn't know what she was agreeing to. She wanted him and she trusted him. Nothing else mattered.

His mouth came down on hers, but this time it was different. Before, there had been passion, but now there was a raw, unchecked power to his kiss. Before, he had explored, but now he plunged. She met him more than halfway and gave back a few thrusts of her own.

He rolled her onto her back and ran one hand up and down her body. His touch was as soft as it had always been, but there was an impulsive quality to the movements, as if he felt rather than thought first. He circled her breasts, then slid his hand down her stomach before slipping his fingers into the protective curls between her thighs.

Everywhere he touched, her skin tightened and her nerve endings burned. She had to cling to him to keep from writhing under the exquisite perfection of what he was doing. When he moved into the sensitive folds of skin, her legs opened and she raised her hips.

"You're so wet," he murmured against her mouth. "I want that. I want you to have trouble breathing or thinking."

He was getting his wish, but it would require air to tell him that so she could only strain and twist as he explored her.

He moved to her opening and gently pushed one finger inside. She was so tight. He groaned against her mouth, then tried two fingers. They both gasped. Heather felt her body slowly stretching back to life. She was too hot, too aroused, too everything, and she never wanted this moment to end.

He continued to pleasure her. At the same time, he kissed her cheek, then her nose, then her jaw. In and out, slowly, deliberately, driving her crazy.

"That's where I want to be," he murmured. "Inside you, filling you. I'm going to make you scream."

She opened her eyes and looked at him. "I believe you."

"Good."

He moved his hand higher, searching for, then finding, that tiny spot of pleasure. She jumped.

"So it's there," he said, stroking it gently. "How do you like it?" His fingers continued their intimate dance. "Like this?" He rubbed over it. "Or like this?" He licked the inside of her ear. "Show me. Take my hand and show me."

Heather hesitated. No one had ever asked her to do that before.

He read her confusion and embarrassment. "So we can be naked together, we can kiss each other, taste each other and perform the most intimate act possible, but you won't put your hand on top of mine to show me what you like?"

Heat flared on her cheeks. "If you insist on being logical, I refuse to do this with you."

"Really?" His voice teased her.

She knew he had a point. It was just so *personal.*

"I'm waiting."

It was then she realized he'd stopped moving his hand. It was still pressing against her but not doing those delicious things. Jim kissed the side of her neck, then moved down to her breasts.

"I want to please you in every possible way," he breathed against her skin. "I want you to lose yourself in the moment. I want to feel you reaching that moment of perfect pleasure against my fingers and I want my tongue in your mouth while it's happening. Let me please you. Show me what you want.''

The ache inside her doubled as he spoke. She trembled with frantic need. It would take so very little to bring her to release, so she shifted her hand until it was on top of his and led him back to her center. There she moved him in a tight circle that teased at her most sensitive spot but didn't brush across it.

''Like that,'' she said.

''Thank you.''

Then he was kissing her deeply, and his fingers were performing magic. Her hand fell away only to, a minute or so later, clutch at his shoulder as her body tightened in anticipation. Her hips rose and fell and she had trouble breathing, but none of that mattered.

Closer and closer he drew her until she was shaking and unbearably tense. He broke the kiss to look at her. Their eyes met and she knew he could see everything she was feeling. Her soul was exposed and she didn't care.

At that moment, he gently stroked the place she most desired. Everything froze as if time had stopped. It was the last whisper of silence before the crash of the storm.

Jim continued to stare at her, then he bent down and plunged inside her mouth as he rapidly and lightly continued to caress her until she exploded in his arms.

The pleasure overwhelmed her. She clung to him to keep from being swept away. She vaguely recalled pulling him closer and gasping, maybe even scream-

ing. She wasn't sure. The intense release drained the
tension from her body. She went limp.

Jim stroked her face and kissed her forehead.
"How would you describe it?"

"Extraordinary. Incredible. Wonderful?"

He looked very pleased with himself, but then he
had every right to be. She'd experienced that ultimate
feeling of ecstasy before, but nothing close to being
in the same league as this. It was as if he'd discovered
a whole new set of nerve endings in her body and
made them all sing hallelujah.

"Did I scream?" she asked.

"Yup."

"I've never screamed before."

"I've never made a woman scream, so we're
even." He gave her a quick kiss. "We have a little
problem."

She reached between them and touched the length
of his arousal. He was hard and ready and his breath
caught as her fingers closed around him. "I wouldn't
say little," she told him. "Not even average. I think
this is a *big* problem."

"Thanks for the compliment, but that's not what I
mean. I don't have any condoms with me, and I assume you're not on birth control."

"I'm not." She cleared her throat. "But I do have,
well, protection."

She tensed, half-waiting for his gaze to turn accusing or for him to recoil with disgust. He did neither.
Instead, he smiled and said, "I like a woman who's
prepared."

"Yeah?"

"Yeah. Where are they?"

She pointed to the nightstand. He opened the drawer and pulled out the small box containing three condoms. The box was still sealed. She'd purchased it in a fit of defiance after Luke had left her but had never had the occasion to use them before. A couple of times, she had nearly thrown them out, but now she was glad she hadn't. They were going to come in very handy.

Jim put on the protection, then shifted until he was between her knees. "I want to be inside you, Heather."

"I want that, too." She stroked his face, tracing the outline of his mouth, then cupped his cheeks.

"I'll take it slow."

The thought of what those words meant had her shivering in anticipation. She wanted him to go slowly, to fill her inch by inch until she thought she might die from the pleasure. Desire swept through her, and it was as if her recent release had never occurred. She wanted him as powerfully as she had before.

"Make love to me," she whispered. "Please."

He braced his weight on his arms, his arousal seeking her feminine place. She reached a hand down between them to guide him in. As promised, he went slowly. Her body stretched and contracted, then stretched again. Her breath caught as wave after wave of incredible need washed through her, leaving her breathless and wanting.

She hadn't realized she could be so ready again so quickly, but as soon as he'd entered her all the way, she felt herself straining toward her completion. He withdrew, and on his next thrust, a rolling wave of release gathered momentum with his withdrawal, then swept over her again. It had never been like this before. She didn't understand what was different, and she couldn't find it in herself to care. There was only the moment and the man. Her body convulsed again and again, drawing him in.

She clung to him, begging him to never stop. He thrust harder and faster until she couldn't stand how wonderful everything was. She wrapped her legs around his hips and kissed him. They shuddered together in one last incredible explosion.

Sometime later, Jim felt the world come into focus around them. Heather was still in his arms, their bodies pressed against each other. He stroked her silky hair and breathed in the scent of their lovemaking.

"That was incredible," he said.

"I know." Satisfaction filled her voice. "I didn't know it could be like that."

"Me neither."

He'd never had a woman respond the way Heather had. He'd never felt so connected and complete...or so terrified. Being in Heather's embrace was like coming home, and that was a sensation he'd spent his whole adult life avoiding. He didn't want to connect. He didn't want to get involved. And it was way too late to be having these concerns now. It had already happened. Somewhere between their first hello in the elevator and their lovemaking today, she had become his absolution.

"How long can we put off the sensible conversation?" she asked.

He knew what she meant. It was one thing for two

consenting adults to agree to make love without promise of a relationship. In that case, sex was a shared biological function that was supposed to make them both feel good when it was over. But that wasn't what had happened this time. They'd gone to a different level and he didn't know how to get back to where they'd been before. What if he couldn't? What if the only place he would ever belong was right here, with her?

"What do you want to do?" he asked.

He wanted her to answer all the questions because he had a bad feeling that if she asked them of him, he would be at risk of telling her what he really felt.

"I want to never move," she said with a laugh, then shifted until she was sitting up.

Her hair was mussed, her face flushed. She was the most beautiful woman he'd ever seen. She reached over the side of the bed and pulled on her short robe.

"Okay, I've moved." She drew in a breath. "I don't know what I want. Actually, the truth is I know what I want and I know what is sensible. The sensible side of me says that we can't be this intimate and still maintain a working relationship. I thought we could, but I underestimated the chemistry."

"Agreed."

Her green eyes darkened. "I don't want to quit my job."

"I don't want you to go."

"I want to stay friends."

"Me, too."

Her mouth twisted into a grimace. "I'm lying through my teeth about all of this."

He knew exactly what she meant. The "right"

thing wasn't what either of them wanted to do. But
that alone convinced him that it had to be done. He
wanted to tell her how much he wanted her. He
wanted to say that even though it would never work
out between them, he'd like to think that it would, at
least for a little while. Instead, he tried to smile.

"One of us has to pretend to be logical so the other
one can pretend to agree," he told her. "We'll fake
it until we're ready to act like it's real." He reached
out and took her hand in his. "I don't want you to
quit, and I don't want to lose your friendship. But we
can't stay lovers and stay uninvolved."

"I don't want love in my life," she said.

"I don't want it, either."

"So we won't make a habit out of this."

"Of course not."

But he didn't want to let go of her fingers and he
very much wanted to pull her close and make love
with her again. He wanted to hear her say that she
loved him and have her beg him to stay. Because if
she did that, he just might be willing to give this all
a chance. Even though he knew it was certain to end
in disaster.

He knew that once he left her apartment, he
wouldn't be able to stop thinking about her. He
couldn't imagine a life without Heather, but he also
knew the kindest act would be to let her go.

She looked at him, then smiled. "You know, it's
not very late. Maybe we could agree to start being
sensible tomorrow." She slipped her robe off her
shoulders. "Unless you're too tired."

Just for the night, he promised himself. He would
return to reality in the morning. Just for now, he

would let himself believe that maybe this time everything was going to be all right.

He reached out and tugged at the belt of her robe. ''I'm not tired at all.''

She glanced down and saw the physical result of her words, then she leaned toward him. ''Maybe this time I could be on top,'' she whispered.

Chapter Thirteen

Heather woke to Diane's crying. She recognized the fussy sound that had become so familiar over the past couple of weeks. Her daughter was still suffering the ill effects of teething. But as Heather sat up and stretched, she couldn't help smiling. Every part of her body ached pleasantly, and although she'd only gotten a few hours of sleep, she felt completely refreshed and ready to face the world. Last night had been the most incredible experience.

She walked into Diane's room and picked her up. "I know you're not feeling well, sweet cheeks, but according to Grandma, you just have a few more days, then you'll be your cheerful self again."

With that, she held her baby close to her chest and twirled around the room. She had an irresistible urge to hum or laugh aloud. She felt like a character in a romantic movie. She wanted to sweep open the windows and call "Good morning" to the birds and squirrels, which would only frighten the poor creatures.

Even Diane seemed to sense her good mood. Her daughter's fussiness quieted and she laughed with her mother as they made a second circuit of the room. Heather took the baby's hand in her own, held out the tiny arm and switched from an oddly gaited waltz to a modified tango. Diane squealed with delight.

It wasn't just that the lovemaking had been so incredible, Heather thought as she set her daughter on the changing table and saw to her diaper. It was that Jim had been such a responsive lover. He'd been tender and serious and playful and caring and how on earth was she supposed to resist that? It wasn't enough that the guy was perfect in every other way. Now she had firsthand proof that he was dynamite in bed.

Thank goodness she'd been smart enough to keep her heart carefully out of reach. If she hadn't, it would have been so easy to fall in love with him. But they'd come together as consenting adults and nothing about their relationship had changed.

Heather bit her lower lip as she wondered if she'd been careful enough. Had she started to think of Jim as more than just her boss and a good friend?

Something stirred in the back of her mind, but she ignored the soft whispers. If it was different, she didn't want to know. Better for both of them if she believed everything was as it had been except for the incredible memories of their night together.

An hour later, she pulled up in front of the office.

Despite her assertions that nothing was different, her heart started beating a little faster as she headed for the front door of the building. Would Jim be inside? What would they say when they saw each other? She was determined to act normally, but she had a sudden apprehension that she wouldn't be able to remember what normal was like.

But when she stepped inside the room, she found that she didn't have anything to worry about. Jim wasn't anywhere to be seen. Heather flashed Flo a smile, called out a friendly greeting and went to settle Diane for the day.

"How's she feeling?" Flo asked as she rose to her feet and came after Heather. "Is she still crying?"

"Most of the time," Heather admitted. "She slept through the night, but I think that was just to gather strength for her second assault. I thought about setting up the playpen in the office. Is that all right with you?"

"You know she's the light of my life. Let's put it by my desk so I'll have an excuse not to work. I can just play with my little princess." She stroked Diane's cheek. "How are you, baby girl? You want to play with your auntie Flo?"

Diane smiled at the familiar face and raised her hands as if indicating she wanted Flo to hold her.

"Do you mind?" Flo asked.

"Be my guest."

Heather set the diaper bag on the floor, then went to get the playpen from the lunchroom. It had been designed for mobility and she had it set up in less than five minutes. After collecting a couple of Diane's favorite toys, she snapped a colorful animal mobile in place, then wound up the attached music box.

"Look at what your mommy did for you," Flo said as she cuddled Diane. "All those toys and a nice, soft place to play. Aren't you a lucky girl?"

In her tight, sleeveless purple blouse and matching capri pants, Flo looked more like a cocktail waitress than a mom, but to Heather, she was all things maternal. Despite the big hair and bigger makeup, she had a warm and loving heart. Heather's chest tightened with sadness and sympathy. Flo accepted her childless state gracefully, but Heather thought it was a tragedy. Flo would have been a terrific mother. She would have loved with her whole being and what child could want more than that?

"I'll be right here," Flo said as she set Diane in the playpen. "Right beside you. Yes, that's right." Then she straightened, looked at Heather and raised her eyebrows. "How was the wild thing?"

Heather blinked in stunned surprise. "Excuse me?"

"You heard me. I was asking about your evening. I know that you and Jim were together. And I mean that in the most intimate sense. So how was it?"

Color heated Heather's cheeks. She pressed her hands to her face and groaned softly. "How did you know? Is it that obvious? Am I wearing a sign or something?"

Flo leaned against her desk. "You're glowing, honey, and it's not because of any new makeup or the fact that you got a good night's sleep. I'd say you didn't get much sleep at all. But if it makes you feel any better, I had a real big hint from Jim this morning.

He's so happy, I would swear he'd seen the second coming, if you'll excuse the pun. I thought the man was going to break out in song.''

Heather couldn't prevent a smile from stealing across her face. So Jim really had enjoyed their time together. Of course, she knew that he had, but it was nice to know he was still floating, too.

Heather walked over to her desk and sat down.

''I won't press you for details,'' Flo went on, ''even though I want to. For one thing, I doubt you'll tell me much. For another, he's my boss and there are some things an employee just shouldn't know.''

''I'm an employee.''

''That's right, honey, and you'll have to work that one out all on your own.''

Heather knew what her friend was talking about. ''I agree. We both talked about it. We can't make it anything more than it was. Yes, we had a lovely time together and it was very special, but we decided that our friendship, not to mention our working relationship, was more important.''

Flo studied her. ''Did you now?''

''Yes. We're both adults. We can handle this.'' Heather felt herself getting a little defensive and she wasn't sure why.

''Whose idea was that?''

''Both of ours. It's what I want. I'm not looking for a man in my life. At least not romantically. I like that Jim and I are friends. If we can keep things at that level, they won't get complicated.''

Flo folded her arms under her impressive bosom. ''Life has a way of complicating things whether we

want it to or not. But it's your call. You two have to
do what's right."

"You don't approve?"

"It's not my place to approve or disapprove. I think
you're whistling in the dark. Most women I know
can't spend the night making love with a wonderful
man and then walk away without a second thought."

Heather knew she was right. "It's not going to be
easy, but it can be done."

"I'm sure it can." Flo glanced down at Diane.
"She's a sweet thing and you're a great mom. But
life is better when there's someone to share the load.
Jim has a good heart and he needs someone to see
that and to love him back."

"I do care about Jim," Heather admitted.

"I'm not talking about friendship caring. I'm talking about the real thing. The love between a man and
a woman. The marrying kind of love. Jim won't be
easy to convince for a lot of reasons, but the woman
who wins him will have a prize worth holding on to.
There aren't many like him."

Fear clutched at Heather's insides. "I don't want
marriage. I don't want to risk falling in love again."

Flo shrugged. "Then I guess you're not the one. I
keep waiting for her to show up and claim him. Lord
knows he needs someone to love him."

"Everyone does," Heather agreed. She told herself
she wasn't the one. She'd been down this road and it
hadn't once worked for her. She didn't want anything
to change between her and Jim. "But I can't fall in
love," she said.

"Nobody is saying you have to."

But Heather felt pressured in ways she couldn't understand. "I thought those other men were terrific, too. All of them. And they turned out to be all wrong for me. How can I trust my judgment about Jim?"

"If those other men were as great as him, then I guess you can't."

Heather wanted to say that they *had* been that wonderful, but she knew there was a difference. She'd never met anyone like Jim before. He was a living, breathing hero and that terrified her. How was she supposed to live up to that? If she tried again with someone like him and it didn't work, then she really wouldn't have any faith in love.

"It's too great a risk," she said slowly. "I'm not willing to take the chance."

Flo grimaced in impatience. "Do you have any idea what you're giving up? All because you're afraid?"

The door to the office opened before Heather could reply. Two policemen entered the room. "We're looking for Brian Johnson," the taller of the two said. "We have a warrant for his arrest."

"What the hell is going on?" Jim demanded when he stormed into the office. He tossed the logbook onto Flo's desk. "When did the police get here?"

Flo's face was pale, the only color coming from the splotches of blusher on her cheeks. She glanced at the clock, then at Heather. "Maybe an hour ago."

He glanced at Heather for confirmation. She nodded. "It was over in a matter of minutes. They checked his identification, read him his rights, then took him away. None of us knew what to say to them or what to do."

He stared at the two frightened women. Heather held little Diane in her arms as if to protect her from all that had happened. Rage and frustration bubbled inside him. What the hell was going on? One minute he'd been flying a couple of executives over to LAX to catch their flight back east and the next Flo had radioed him with the news that Brian had been arrested for dealing drugs.

He raked his fingers through his hair and paced to his desk. "There's nothing you could have done. They had a warrant for his arrest. You couldn't have stopped them. I'm just sorry I wasn't here." Not that he could have done anything, either.

"They searched his locker for drugs," Heather said quietly.

Jim turned to her. "Did they have a warrant for that?"

She nodded. "Several other police officers arrived as they were taking him away. They didn't find anything. They're going to be in touch with you later. I think they want to search the whole place."

This wasn't happening, he thought grimly. It couldn't be. "How could I have been so wrong about that kid?" he asked, not expecting an answer. He thought he knew Brian.

Heather crossed to Flo's desk and handed her the baby, then she moved next to him. "Something's not right," she said firmly. "We all know Brian. He's a bright, sweet kid and I don't think he's involved with drugs. Maybe I'm a fool, but I don't think so." She frowned. "The police said they had an anonymous tip from a witness. Someone who knew Brian's name and where he worked. Even if he was involved with something like that, he's too smart to get caught that way. Some kind of police operation, like a sting or something, would make sense, but not this.''

"She's right," Flo said. "You're going to have to do something."

What he wanted to do was forget he'd ever met the kid. But Heather's words rang true. Some of the rage cleared out of his brain and he was able to think. "Brian wants to fly helicopters," he said slowly. "That's all he talks about. He has a steady girlfriend he's devoted to and he gets good grades in school."

"Exactly," Heather said. "When he's not with her or at school, he's here. When would he have the time? You have to go talk to him."

He looked at her, then cupped her cheek. "You're right, I do."

The second his hand touched her soft skin, he was reminded of all that had happened the night before. Of the way they'd made love over and over. This was not the morning greeting he'd planned. But they had more pressing matters than their personal life, and he wasn't about to say anything intimate in front of Flo.

He grabbed his car keys from his desk and headed for the door. "I'll call when I know anything," he said as he left.

It took some fast talking, but the police finally let him speak to Brian. Jim was ushered into a small room with no windows and only one door. A worn table surrounded by three chairs nearly filled the small space. He had to wait thirty minutes until the door opened and Brian was led inside.

The teenager was still in his own clothes—a T-shirt and jeans—but there the similarities to the young man

he knew ended. The boy was pale and obviously terrified. Tears streaked his face. He was shaking and
smelled as if he'd recently thrown up. And handcuffs
bound his bony wrists. He looked young and alone
and scared.

"I can't believe you're here," Brian said, his voice
trembling. "I didn't think you'd come."

Jim noticed the boy wouldn't meet his eyes.
"When a trusted employee of mine is arrested for
something, I want to know the story."

Tears spilled down Brian's face. "I never did drugs
in my life. Never. I swear. I didn't even once try pot.
I've seen too many people killed by that s-stuff." His
voice cracked. "Jeez, I wouldn't sell them, either. It's
not just wrong, it's stupid." He sniffed and finally
raised his gaze to meet Jim's. "Someone set me up."

Jim wasn't sure what he'd expected the kid's story
to be, but he hadn't thought it would be that. "Someone set you up? Why?"

He heard the skepticism in his voice. Brian did, too.
He slumped back in his chair and shook his head.
"What does it matter? You're not going to believe
me. No one is. I'm just some punk kid, right? No
dad, no important family, no money. No one cares."

But Jim knew that he *did* care—very much. Brian
was lost and didn't know which way to turn.

Jim leaned forward, resting his hands on the rickety
table. "Tell me who set you up, and why?"

Brian raised his shackled hands and swiped at his
tears. "Bernie."

Jim straightened in surprise. "The charter pilot?"
He pictured the short, hard-edged man. "He's a pain

in the neck, but why would he do something like that?''

Brian's pale face flooded with color. ''I caught him in the hangar. He was using one of the helicopters as a hotel room. It happened a couple of times. The first time, I didn't say anything, but the second, I told him I was going to tell you. He said if I did, he would make me pay big time.'' He gave a sob. ''That was last week.''

Jim swore loudly. Bernie wasn't his favorite guy in the world and one of the reasons was that the pilot liked to live life a little too close to the edge. He'd been reprimanded for unsafe flying a couple of times and had a reputation for hard drinking and lots of women. With any other pilot, Brian's story would have been crazy, but with Bernie it could be true.

Jim rose to his feet. ''I don't know how long this will take, so you'll have to sit tight. I know a couple of lawyers. I'll call one of them and find out who I talk to first. You might have to spend the night here, but I will get you out, Brian. Don't worry.''

''You believe me?''

''Sure. Why wouldn't I?''

Fresh tears spilled down Brian's cheeks. ''No one ever has before.''

Jim felt an uncomfortable tightness in his chest. He pulled the boy to his feet and hugged him. ''Well, I do, and I'll make damn sure that Bernie gets what's coming to him.''

As Jim hugged him goodbye, harsh, shuddering sobs tore through his thin body. ''I was so scared,'' Brian said, his voice muffled against Jim's jacket.

"I know. Believe me, I know about being scared. Don't worry, I won't tell anyone."

The teenager sniffed and looked up. "Thanks. I wouldn't want Heather thinking I was, you know, a wimp."

"She doesn't. In fact, she believed in you from the beginning."

"Yeah?"

Jim smiled to himself. So the seventeen-year-old had a crush on Heather. He couldn't blame him. What man wouldn't be tempted by such an alluring woman?

He ruffled the boy's hair. "Hang tight, and I'll get back to you as soon as I know something. With a little luck, we'll have you out first thing in the morning."

"I can't believe you got him out the same day," Heather said later that night. She tucked the phone between her ear and her shoulder and shifted Diane so the baby could rest against her. It was nearly ten in the evening and her daughter was drifting off to sleep.

"Everything fell into place," Jim said. "The authorities thought there was something odd about the tip, but with all the planted evidence, they had no choice but to take him in. When they searched Bernie's apartment, they found drugs and a record book. Apparently, he's been doing this for years."

"It's amazing the man could still fly."

"Scary is more like it," Jim told her. "The police want to search the facility to see if he stored drugs there, but we're not considered part of the investigation."

"What happened when you confronted him?"

"He crumpled like a wet sheet."

Heather smiled as she heard the satisfaction in Jim's voice. "You're so big on beating people up, I'm surprised you didn't want to take him behind the building," she teased.

"It crossed my mind, but I like to consider that a last resort. Besides, I prefer the idea of his being in prison for a long time."

"Brian came by to see us," she said, remembering the disbelieving but thrilled expression on the boy's face. "He couldn't get over the fact that we believed in him."

"He's got a crush on you," Jim said.

"I know. But you're the one he's going to worship now. I think he'd change the rotation of the earth if you asked him to."

"I like things the way they are." Jim sounded uncomfortable. "All I want him to do is get good grades in school and show up for work on time."

She could imagine him shifting in his chair, a little embarrassed by Brian's gratitude and very happy to have been able to help the boy.

"I don't think you have to worry about Brian. In his mind, he has something to prove. He wants you to know that he's worthy of your trust, so I predict we'll be seeing a straight-A student this year."

"That's not a bad thing," Jim said. He was quiet for a second. "I keep thinking about how hard this was on him. He's too young to have to wrestle with this sort of thing. I can't believe Bernie threatened him. I know Brian feels guilty for not coming to me right away, but I understand why he was scared. It would be his word against Bernie's. Brian was the new guy, and a kid, while Bernie was a supposedly trusted pilot.''

"What a dilemma," Heather agreed, thinking that Jim had had his share of impossible situations.

Many people said the past didn't matter, but Heather didn't agree with them. She believed everyone carried around pieces of their past and that they were the reason for certain ways of behaving. She still hadn't figured out all the ways Jim was reacting to his past, but he was still afraid to connect, afraid to love.

"You all right?" Jim asked.

"Fine."

"You're quiet."

"I'm just thinking about everything that's happened." She glanced at the clock. "I know it's late, but would you like to come over?" She hesitated, remembering what had happened the previous evening. "This isn't necessarily an invitation into my bed as much as a desire to be with a good friend. I think I need that right now."

She wanted to see him and hold him and have him tell her that everything was going to be all right. She wanted to know that what they'd shared the previous night had mattered to him as much as it had mattered to her.

"Thanks, Heather, but I can't. As you said, it's late. I still have some work to catch up on before I can go to sleep. I'll see you in the morning. Bye."

He was gone. She stared at the receiver, not quite able to believe that he'd hung up on her. Just like that. She wasn't sure what it meant, but she didn't like it. There had been something odd about his voice. Something that made her wonder if there was a problem between them.

Had their becoming lovers changed everything? Had they crossed that line and was there no going back? Or was it something else? Was it about Brian and what he'd faced? Had Brian's fears mirrored Jim's own until he felt compelled to run and hide from her?

Was this the secret she'd been searching for? Was this the reason Jim had never married or even been seriously involved with a woman? Fear of his past? Fear that he wouldn't be enough?

And how on earth was she supposed to be able to break through that particular barrier? Flo had said he was worth fighting for. Heather agreed. But there wouldn't be much of a battle if one of the participants refused to show up.

Chapter Fourteen

"**Y**ou're avoiding me," Heather said nearly two weeks later as she and Jim settled on her sofa. They had just enjoyed their first dinner together since the night they'd made love. "At first I thought you just weren't speaking to me, but then it became pretty obvious you were avoiding me completely."

She'd practiced half a dozen opening lines, some funny, some charming, but in the end had decided on the truth. It had taken her a couple of days to figure out what was going on. In the trauma of dealing with the aftermath of Brian's arrest and having the police search the hangar, it had been easy to let everything else go. But then she'd realized that the easy companionship she'd taken for granted had disappeared so completely it was as if it had never been.

She couldn't believe Jim had changed so much.

Then she'd noticed him watching her when he thought she wasn't looking. There had been something almost lost in his vulnerable gaze, and that unnamed, but pain-filled expression had persuaded her to step back and get a little perspective on the situation.

Obviously, making love had been the catalyst for this change between them. There had been a fundamental shift in how they thought about each other and now they had two choices. They could either accept the change and go on from there, or they would have to work very hard to return to where they'd been before. Heather couldn't decide what she wanted, but after a while that had ceased to matter. What was most important was that she'd lost a special friendship in her life. First she had to find out if there was a way to get it back.

Jim angled toward her on the sofa. His gaze settled on her face and he studied her as if seeing her for the first time. She stared at his strong jawline, the firm yet tender mouth, the expressive eyes and dark hair. As she catalogued features that had become both familiar and dear, she wondered what she was going to do if he told her he didn't want to be friends anymore. Her life, which had recently seemed so satisfying and abundant, would grow a little smaller and colder.

She thought he might be angry, but instead he smiled at her. "I see you don't believe in polite conversation first," he said. "You just jump straight to the point."

"Our dinner was one of polite conversation."

"I suppose it was." He drew in a breath. "You're right. I have been avoiding you. It wasn't the most intelligent or sensitive way to handle the situation, but I didn't know what else to do.''

At least she hadn't been imagining things. ''Because we made love.'' She wasn't asking a question.

He nodded. ''We both agreed that it was a one-time thing and that nothing else would change, but it's not that simple.'' He grimaced. ''I can't stop thinking about what happened. I want to be with you again. But I know that would screw everything up and our relationship is too important to me. I want you in my life. I want us to be friends, and yet I don't want to hurt you. Until I could figure out how to make it work, it somehow seemed easier to avoid you.'' He reached out and touched her hand. ''That was selfish and shortsighted. I'm sorry.''

She didn't answer him right away, mostly because she couldn't decide what issue to address first. He couldn't stop thinking about their being together? Her heart fluttered in her chest. She had the same problem. Memories were keeping her up nights and she couldn't afford to lose the sleep. She was also wrestling with the issue of maintaining their friendship.

She wanted to move close to him and hug him. She wanted to beg him to make love with her. She wanted to make him promise that, no matter what, he would never again disappear from her life.

''Thank you for being honest,'' she said at last. ''I was afraid you didn't want to be friends with me anymore. I was afraid you wanted me out of your life.''

''Never.'' His fingers curled around her wrist. ''But I don't want to hurt you.''

It was one of those rare statements that rang with sincerity. She sensed he was being completely honest.

He genuinely was more concerned with her feelings than his own. She felt a flood of warm contentment flow through her.

"You couldn't," she assured him.

His gaze narrowed. "You're wrong, Heather. I could hurt you very much, even though I don't want to. Please remember that. Whatever happens, I'll never hurt you on purpose."

She shivered involuntarily. "What does that mean?"

"Just what I said."

But before she could pursue that line of questioning, Diane began fussing in her playpen. Jim rose and gathered her to him.

"How's my best little girl?" he asked as he cradled her in his arms. Her restlessness quieted instantly. "Feeling better?"

Diane had spent the past several days battling an ear infection.

"The doctor says she's doing great," Heather said. "Apparently, a lot of kids get this, but she doesn't seem prone, thank goodness. But all the medicine and sleeplessness has messed up her schedule just after we'd gotten back on track."

"That's all right. You'll start another schedule, won't you, sweet cheeks?"

His voice was low, soft, and to Heather at least, very seductive. Or maybe it was just the sight of this tall, strong man holding a small baby in his arms. Jim gazed at Diane with all the love and devotion of a father, and in many ways, that's what he was whether he realized it or not.

"Pretty, pretty girl," he said to Diane as he carried

her around the room. "You are so lucky. You're going to have a wonderful life. When you're six or seven, you'll have a bike and suddenly you'll be able to go places. Having your own wheels is a very cool thing. When you're ten, you can have a horse, and by the time you're thirteen, you'll be a beauty just like your mother."

Heather opened her mouth to say she hoped her daughter would be much more attractive, then closed it. There was no point in sharing her insecurities about her own appearance with a man who would never, by virtue of his gender, understand.

"All the boys will have crushes on you," he went on. "I can tell. You're going to be a heartbreaker."

"Did you have a crush on a girl when you were thirteen?" she asked.

He looked at her and shrugged. "No. I didn't discover girls until a couple of years later, although most of my friends had by that age."

"You don't strike me as a late bloomer."

"I wasn't, but at thirteen I didn't have time to be a kid. I was too busy taking care of my mother."

He continued to croon to Diane, then said he would put her to bed for the night.

Heather nodded weakly. She couldn't speak. She'd heard the truth before and thought she'd understood what he was saying, but now she realized that, until this exact minute, she hadn't absorbed the reality of all that Jim had been through.

There were no secrets to Jim Dyer. She'd seen through to his soul. She knew his demons and how they preyed upon him and he was still the best man she'd ever known. He was everything that he appeared to be—warm, loving, caring…and terrified that it was never going to be enough. He lived in fear that he wouldn't be able to fix whatever problems life gave him in his personal relationships, so he avoided them rather than fail again. Because to him, failure meant death. First the death of his mother, then the death of his child.

She walked into her bedroom and turned on the lamp. After pulling back the covers, she took off her clothes, then waited.

It only took a few minutes for Jim to settle Diane. He walked out into the hall and glanced into her room. She stood naked in the soft lamplight. He stopped as suddenly as if he'd run into a wall and just stared. She might have been scared…okay, she *was* scared, but the bulge in his trousers told her that she hadn't completely misjudged the situation.

"I need you," she said quietly. "Please make love with me."

His own need had become a tangible beast. Jim could feel its hot breath on the back of his neck. How the hell was he supposed to resist her? Even in a potato sack, Heather would be tempting enough to lead a saint astray, but now, naked and vulnerable, she was irresistible. Especially to him.

He told himself it was a mistake. He told himself this was a place he couldn't afford to go. Once he made love to her again, there was no going back. He would lose himself in her and then he would be lost forever. But he couldn't resist her. Perhaps she'd been sent to him as a test. If so, he was going to fail, but in the most glorious way possible.

He crossed to her in three long strides, then drew

her into his arms and kissed her. There were so many sensations, each better than the last. He savored the taste of her sweet mouth and the way she opened to welcome him. Her tongue brushed against his, sending pleasure jolting through him. Her body was soft, warm and yielding. He traced familiar curves along her back, her sides and her rear. He cupped her and she surged against him, pressing her belly against his arousal.

He wanted her more than he had before. This time he knew what kind of paradise awaited him between her legs. He knew how tight and wet she could be, how she could start to climax well before he was ready and that each ripple of her release would bring him closer until he plunged into her, spilling himself, feeling her muscles contract again and again around him. He knew how they would hold on to each other in the aftermath as their breathing returned to normal. He knew how an unnamed emotion would tease at the corners of his mind, tempting him with the one thing he could never have. He knew how he would have to leave her and that the leaving would nearly bring him to his knees.

Even knowing what it would cost him later, even knowing that the sensible thing would be to walk away, he couldn't. Perhaps if she hadn't been naked. No, that wouldn't have been enough. Perhaps if they hadn't been alone together in the house. Was that the real reason he'd been avoiding her? That having once made love with her, he couldn't be with her again without needing that intimacy as much as he needed to breathe?

The answer didn't matter, he decided, giving himself over to the sensation of her slenderness in his arms. She was here and she wanted him. If he died later, so be it.

Her eager fingers tugged at the buttons of his shirt. He let her unfasten them as he kissed her jaw, then moved to lick the inside of her perfect ear. She giggled against his chest as she wrestled with the buttons.

"I can't concentrate when you do that," she said.

"Is that so bad?"

"Yes."

He paused long enough to shed his shirt, jeans, boots, socks and underwear. Then he was as naked as she was.

He put his hands on her waist and urged her to lie down. But when she lay on her back, he told her to turn over.

"What are you going to do to me?" she asked as she settled her head on her folded arms and looked at him through the curtain of her blond hair.

"Nothing you won't like," he promised.

Her more subtle curves were still new to him, and while he'd always found joy in the softness of breasts, hips and buttocks, there was an ethereal beauty in Heather's slightness. Other men might not take the time to notice the perfect porcelain quality of her skin or the fact that her small breasts were exquisitely sensitive. She was his prize...his princess...and he was grateful for her generosity in allowing him to be with her.

He straddled her thighs, then bent over and pushed her hair away from the back of her neck. Then he kissed the tender curve and felt her catch her breath.

"That tickles," she whispered. "But in a good way. Don't stop."

If he had his way, he would never stop, he thought as he kissed and nibbled and licked down her spine. He ran his hands along her sides, the long, smooth strokes a counterpoint to the shivery touch of his mouth and tongue. When he reached her waist, he shifted so that he could lick the backs of her knees. She started suddenly and gave a tiny scream. He pinned her with his greater weight and strength so she could only wriggle but not escape.

"Jim, please."

"Stop?"

"No. Never. I want…" He gently bit her rear and her breath caught. Her sentence died in an exhale of delight. "What are you doing to me?"

Making you mine. But he didn't say that. He just turned her over and went to work on her ankles.

From toes to thighs, he touched and licked and kissed until she was tossing her head and begging him to stop, not to stop, to please just touch her *there*. But he didn't. He avoided the heat and sweetness of her, even though the very thought of it made him throb. If she even brushed against him, he would have exploded against her, spilling himself like a seventeen-year-old boy. Tasting and smelling her, learning what made her moan and cry out and sigh was the most perfect experience of his life. He wanted to know all of her. He wanted to know her better than anyone ever had before. He wanted to learn the details, the tiny, nearly insignificant things that would make her come apart in his arms.

When he'd discovered all he could about her legs,

he shifted so he could kiss her mouth. As his lips pressed against hers, she wrapped her arms around him and hauled him close. She was insistent. She attacked, plunging inside him, nipping him, pulling him closer and slipping one leg between his so she could rub herself against his thigh.

She was wet and hot and all things wonderful. He wanted to bury himself inside her right then, but it was too soon. He wanted more for her.

So he broke the kiss and licked his way down to her belly, then lower to the dark blond curls, damp and glistening with desire. Her legs fell open in anticipation.

"I in no way take responsibility for anything I'm about to say," she said, her voice low and breathless. "I know it's going to be incredible. Just please catch me when I fall."

"Always," he promised, and pressed his tongue against her most sensitive point.

Her upper body came up off the bed and she gave a strangled moan. He loved that tiny place, circling it, licking around it in a slowly steady rhythm. She tasted salty and sweet, so uniquely herself. He could feel the muscles in her legs clenching and unclenching. It was as if he was connected to her and could feel what she felt. He knew how fast, how often, and even before she thought how much she would like it, he slipped a single finger inside her and pressed up.

He stroked her from the inside with a rhythm matching what he did with his tongue. The response was instant. Her entire body clenched, then released in a series of spasms as she climaxed. Her feminine core clamped down on his fingers, contracting over and over, drawing him in, massaging him. He continued to lick that tiny bud, moving faster and lighter until she sagged back against the bed in consummate surrender.

When she was finally still, he moved until he was next to her. She turned into his arms and he held her close. Several more shudders rippled through her and she breathed his name with each one.

"Not bad," she said at last.

He chuckled. "Now there's an endorsement. Would you be willing to say it was nice?"

"Very nice. It was as if you knew what I was feeling even before I did, then responded to that."

"I did."

He hoped she wouldn't ask him to explain it because he didn't have any answers. It had never happened to him before and he doubted it would happen again.

Her warm hand brushed against his chest and moved lower until she encircled him. She propped her chin on his shoulder and looked into his face. "I want to do to you what you did to me. The kissing all over your body, the touching. It was incredible. But I read this article."

He was having trouble concentrating on her words, especially when her fingers were teasing the top of his erection, circling around the sensitive head and running up and down the length. "Uh-huh."

"The article said that once a man thinks he's going to have sex, all he cares about is his..." She paused delicately. "His, well, organ being inside the woman. That if there is any foreplay for him, it's this voice in his head screaming, 'Touch it, touch it, touch it.' Is that true?''

Despite how much he wanted to be inside her, he had to grin. ''That about sums it up.''

She sighed. ''I was afraid of that. So I won't bother with all that unnecessary kissing and nibbling. I'll just tell you that I want you inside me right now.''

She turned toward her nightstand and pulled out a condom, then opened the package. He fumbled with the protection, his need making his fingers tremble. Then she was on her back with her legs spread and he was entering her, nearly gasping at her wet heat and the way he fitted her so perfectly.

His tension increased by the second. ''I'm too close,'' he gasped.

''It's okay. Just go for it.''

Her choice of words made him smile. ''Not yet.''

Even though his entire body screamed in protest, he pulled out of her and rubbed himself against her pleasure point. Her breath caught instantly. She pulled her knees back, and when he slipped she moved him so that his steady strokes hit just the right spot. Then she was pushing him inside her. As he entered, he felt the first ripple of her release.

''I'm coming,'' she breathed against his mouth as he ducked his head to kiss her. ''Every time you move inside me. It's too wonderful. I can't do this for very long.''

''That's not going to be a problem.''

Her spasms added to the friction. Tiny massages accompanied every thrust. Less than a minute later, he came in an explosion so incredibly powerful that he couldn't move, couldn't breathe, couldn't do anything but be in her and feel every cell in his body shudder with the experience.

Later, when they'd taken the time to slip under the covers, he pulled her close to his side. She rested one arm on his chest and slid her knee over his thigh. They fitted together perfectly, he thought, trying to keep himself emotionally distant even as he felt himself tumbling into the dark pit of wanting and needing. He wanted to get as far away from her as he could, but it was too late. It didn't matter how much he traveled or for how long. He'd connected with her and now there would be hell to pay.

He closed his eyes, but that couldn't blot out the truth. He'd crossed his own private line and gone into the place he'd promised himself he would never go. He should have kept his distance. He should have done a thousand things differently. He'd been a fool.

Heather sighed. "I love you."

She spoke the words quietly and easily, as if she'd said them a thousand times before. As if they weren't powerful enough to shake and crumble the foundations of his world. He couldn't respond—he could barely breathe. Love? No. Not possible. His mind and heart rejected the possibility.

"I don't want you to say anything back," she added. "I wasn't even sure I was going to tell you. It kind of slipped out. Nothing will change. I swear, I won't get all weird on you—it's just that I wanted you to know."

She gave a little laugh and looked at him. "This wasn't supposed to happen. After all, I've been very clear on my three-strikes rule. I thought I was done

with love forever. But I can't resist you. Not only
because the lovemaking is so terrific or because you
make a habit of acting like a hero, but because of
how you make me feel when I'm around you. I love
how you look out for me and Diane and how kind
you are and how smart and funny. We'll still be
friends. I promise. But I do love you."

Then she did the most amazing thing. She closed
her eyes and drifted off to sleep.

Jim told himself to stay calm. He held her gently
for over an hour, listening to the sound of her
breathing, replaying her words and trying to figure out
what they meant.

He wanted to believe. What man wouldn't sell his
soul to have a woman like her in his life? He wanted
to respond in kind and tell her that somehow they
would make it work. But he couldn't. Because she
wasn't telling the truth. She couldn't love him. No
one loved him. Not ever. No one got that close. He'd
designed his life to keep the world at bay. What made
her think she could slip past the barriers and find her
way to his heart?

It was all he could do not to shake her awake and
shout at her, telling her that he didn't want her love.
Instead, he slipped out of her bed like the snake that
he was and made his way into the living room. There
he dressed, then left the quiet house. When he closed
the door behind him, he promised himself that he was
never going back inside.

Heather woke and found herself alone in the bed.
At first she thought Jim was somewhere else in the
apartment, but as she walked through the living room,

she realized he was gone. A cold shiver rippled down her spine. Why hadn't he told her he was leaving?

Her feeling of uneasiness persisted through the morning as she got Diane ready, then drove to the office. What had happened? Had he been so disgusted by her confession that he'd had to leave? Had she been wrong to admit her feelings?

"Don't panic," she told herself. "Everything is fine. There's a perfectly logical explanation why he left. He probably just didn't want to be seen walking out of the apartment first thing in the morning."

That had to be it. She'd meant what she said last night. That while she did love him, she didn't expect that fact to fundamentally change their relationship. Or was she fooling herself? Heather stopped at a red light and bit her lower lip. She was willing to admit that in the back of her mind, she had sort of hoped that Jim might respond in kind and open up a discussion about...what? she asked herself. Their future? Did they have a future? Did she want one?

She searched her heart as she drove. Did she want to risk loving a man all over again? Did she want to go through the pain and suffering and the potential for heartbreak, all in the name of love?

She pictured Jim's face as he held her daughter. She remembered his determination to help Brian, and the way he laughed and that silly dimple that made her thighs go up in flames. She thought of how thoughtful he was and the gentleness in his hands and his voice and his heart.

Yes, she did want to risk it all.

The office was empty when she arrived. Flo was probably in one of the hangars checking on flight records. Heather settled Diane, then made her way to her own desk and sat down. A stack of papers lay where she'd left them. Jim had put an envelope on top.

Frowning, she opened it, then read the tersely worded three-line message. In it he told her that he'd found her a different part-time job. The hours were just as flexible, but the pay was better and she started work on Monday.

She scanned it twice in disbelief. He was getting rid of her, just like he got rid of everyone else in his life.

Chapter Fifteen

The first sob tore at Heather like a great monster. She tried to hold back, to gain some kind of control, but the shock was too great. She could only sink into her chair and wonder why this was happening. She'd known that Jim would have some problems accepting the fact that she loved him, but she'd thought he might go into a panic mode and list the fifty-seven reasons why they couldn't be a couple. She hadn't anticipated he would toss her out of his life. The pain was so sharp it hurt to breathe.

"What's wrong?"

Heather looked up and saw Flo standing in front of her desk. She hadn't heard the other woman come into the office.

"Is it Diane?"

Heather reached for a tissue. She shook her head,

then handed her friend the note. "He wants me to go."

Flo scanned the message, then sank into the chair next to Heather's desk. "Okay. Take a deep breath and start at the beginning. What happened?"

"Nothing. Everything. I told him I loved him." Another sob caught in her throat. She wiped her face and gave Flo a brief account of the events from the previous evening. "I can't believe I said it, and now he wants me to leave, just like that."

Flo leaned forward and squeezed her hand. "He doesn't want you to go. The man can be as thick as a board sometimes, especially when it comes to things like this, but you can't take him seriously."

Heather's stomach churned. She thought she might be sick. "How else can I take it?"

"The way he meant it. He's scared. He's reacting, not thinking. Do you really believe that man wants you to go?" Flo's full red lips pulled into a straight line. "You can still turn this all around, but it's going to take some work. Jim won't make it easy. Not for one second. So what you have to decide is what it's worth to you. How far are you willing to go to be with this man?"

"I don't know," Heather admitted. "I can't help thinking I've been a fool for love—again. I should have learned my lesson by now, but I ignored all the warnings. I feel like Jim pulled me in and made me think he was this incredibly perfect man. At least with the others, I knew they were flawed. But I thought he was a real, live hero."

"Is that who you fell in love with?" Flo asked. "A hero? Is that what you need him to be? I thought you were interested in the man." She rose to her feet. "If what you're looking for is a hero, then he's better off without you.''

Heather stared in stunned astonishment. Flo's words stung like salt in an open wound. Anger flared. ''You're certainly quick to write me off,'' she snapped. ''I guess you and Jim really are two of a kind. I don't know why I didn't see it before. To answer your question, although I don't know why I'm bothering, no, I don't need or want Jim to be a hero. I want him to be an ordinary man. Because of all he's done, I forgot that he's just like everyone else. I thought he was perfect, or at least perfect for me. I knew he had some reluctance to getting involved, but then, doesn't everyone? My sense of betrayal comes from the realization that not only wasn't he going to love me back, but he'd also let my feelings for him drive him away. I thought he was capable of growing and changing, and he's not. At least not with me. He would rather be right and safe—and alone—than risk love.''

Flo smiled and leaned back against the chair. ''Well, why didn't you just say so?''

Heather stared in outrage. ''You were testing me?''

''Not exactly. I was trying to figure out how much you cared. You love the man.''

''Of course I do. I said that.''

''There are many different kinds of love. You said you told him that you still wanted to be friends, but it's more than that, isn't it?''

Heather hadn't been willing to admit that to Jim last night, and she wasn't sure she wanted to admit it to Flo now. But there didn't seem to be any point in avoiding the obvious. ''Yes, it's more. I love him as a friend, but I also love him romantically. I want to be with him, always.''

''We're talking marriage?''

''I don't know. Maybe. Yes. I guess.''

Flo grinned. ''I'm so happy for you.'' Then her smile faded. ''The problem is, he won't believe you love him because never once in his life has anyone tried to fight for him. When things got tough, everyone walked away.''

Heather knew that Flo was talking about romantic relationships that she'd observed in the past, but she, Heather, knew a greater truth—about what had happened with Jim's mother and with his high school girlfriend. Flo's words were more true than she realized. No one *had* fought for him, or loved him enough. Not once. If she was right and he believed that failure was death, it was no wonder that he was running from her and any feelings he might have for her.

''You'll have to be the one to make him see the light,'' Flo continued. ''You're going to have to stand up to him.''

''I know you're right, but how?'' Heather picked up the letter. ''He wants me out of his life.''

''Does he? Or is he just afraid to believe what you told him?''

Heather didn't have an answer to that.

''Do you really want him?'' Flo asked.

Heather stared at her friend and smiled. She brushed the last of her tears from her cheeks. ''Oh, yes. I do. I love him. He's kind and honorable. He does the right thing even when it's not the easy thing. He's a good father figure for Diane. He adores her. I suspect he loves her even if he won't admit it. He's smart, he's stubborn and he can be really annoying at times, but that's okay because I can be, too. It's not that I think I may not find anyone better, it's that I'm not interested in anyone else. Jim is my match, my soul mate, and I never thought I'd say that again.''

"So what are you going to do?"

There was only one answer. "Fight for him."

Flo touched the note. "You can start by telling him you're not leaving."

She hadn't thought about refusing to take the other job, but as soon as Flo said it, the advice made perfect sense. Jim wasn't firing her—and she knew he wouldn't. He was simply offering her a different place of employment. She could just as easily turn down his offer.

She wrote "Thanks but no thanks" across the bottom of his letter, then placed it in the center of his desk. When she returned to her seat, she looked at Flo. "Now what?"

"Now you wait."

Easier said than done, Heather thought nearly a week later. No doubt about it, Jim was avoiding her again. She hadn't been in the office when he returned and read her reply to his note. But when she'd next seen him, he hadn't mentioned it. Instead, he'd greeted her politely, as if she were a delivery person, and quickly left. They'd been playing the same game for six days. A noncommittal greeting, polite chitchat and nothing else. He hadn't called, hadn't come over and certainly hadn't in any way acknowledged that they had once been close friends and lovers.

Heather held her sleepy daughter and moved back and forth in the rocking chair in the tiny nursery at

work. The relaxing motion helped her think while
having the added benefit of making Diane drowsy.

"What do you think, sweet cheeks?" she asked
softly. "Is Uncle Jim making you as crazy as he's
making me?"

The man should be shot. If stubbornness and an
inability to see what was right in front of his nose
were a crime, he would be in for life. She knew he
cared a lot. Not just about her but about her daughter.
She knew that he had to miss them as much as they
missed him. The irony was, of course, that if she had
a big crisis in her life, he would be at her side in a
hot minute. But as long as he thought she was strong
and self-sufficient, he would avoid her.

So she waited. For him to figure out the truth. For
him to start to believe that she really loved him. But
would he ever be willing to trust her? He felt the two
most important women in his life had failed him and
was convinced he'd let them down, too.

"I'm afraid he won't give me a try," Heather whispered. "I'm afraid we're going to miss out on what
could have been very wonderful."

She'd already thought of and discarded a dozen
plans, outlined twice that many conversations, all in
the name of persuading him to see how great they
could be together. But she couldn't force him. He
knew her as well as anyone ever had. She'd told him
she loved him. Either he would believe her or he
wouldn't.

So for now, she waited. Waited and prayed and
hoped and loved one very difficult, stubborn, wonderful man.

Jim stared at the quarterly report in front of him,
but it didn't make any sense. He supposed part of the

reason was that he hadn't slept more than a couple of hours a night in the past two weeks. He wasn't eating, either. He couldn't do anything but avoid Heather.

He wasn't even doing that very well. Because not seeing her, but spending all his time thinking about her and missing her, was just as bad as being with her. Except if he only thought about her, he was tempted to touch her or hold her. And if he held her, he might have to ask her if she'd meant what she said when she told him she loved him.

Love. He couldn't understand how she'd just said the word. As if it was easy. It couldn't be easy. It was too powerful and potentially dangerous. So he'd had to let her go because letting go was the only thing that made sense. The only other alternative was to marry her and he could never do that.

"Jim?"

He looked up and stared. It was as if he'd conjured her up from his very thoughts. She stood in front of his desk. So beautiful, so alive. The morning sunlight made her blond hair shine like gold. Diane gurgled from her arms, then saw him and squealed. He hadn't been spending enough time with the baby. He missed her as much as he missed her mother.

"I have a meeting," he said by way of dismissal.

Her smile told him she didn't believe him for a second, but she played along. "This won't take much time. Or maybe it will. I promised myself I'd wait until you were ready, but it's been two weeks, and I'm out of patience. Besides, I've been having this conversation with you in my head daily and I'm finally ready to actually have it with you."

She glanced over her shoulder as though checking

to see if they were alone. She didn't have to worry. Flo had left for the post office and wouldn't be back for half an hour.

"I know your deep, dark secret," she said, her green eyes wide and her gaze direct. "You've spent your entire life trying to fix everything to make up for the fact that you couldn't fix your mom when she was dying. You couldn't convince your girlfriend that the two of you could make it when she was pregnant. Then your mom died and your baby died. And you were left alone both times, standing in the middle of a tragedy with no one to hold you or help you through that living hell of pain and sorrow. So you fix and you fix and you fix because you keep hoping that one day it's finally going to be enough."

His mind screamed at him to run, but he couldn't move. It was like having a bright light glaring down into the small, wizened imperfection that was his soul. She had figured it all out. She was right about everything and he was ashamed.

Her tone softened as she continued. "I have news for you, Jim. You're never going to make up for that past. First, because what's done is done. You can't change that. Second, you weren't the one who was wrong. You were a child and your mother was sick. You wanted to make her better. But you weren't a doctor or God. You were a little boy. You had no power. What she asked of you was wrong."

He didn't respond. He couldn't. He could only stare at her and wonder how long this torture would go on. He'd never wanted her to know this about him. He'd wanted her to believe the facade he showed the world. How could she bear to see him for who and what he was? Didn't it disgust her?

"As far as I'm concerned, you're the greatest guy in the world," she said with a smile. "I wanted to resist you, but who can resist a guy who is so incredibly perfect? Except you're *not* perfect, and that's what I didn't see at first. I kept looking for the flaws. At least with other men, the flaws are usually pretty obvious. But not with you. You hid the truth and I ended up believing in a shadow."

She shifted Diane so that the baby was up against her shoulder. "You keep everyone at arm's length by being the one who takes care of them. A person can respect his mentor but not get that close. You bring them on board, then move them out before they get too important. That way, you're never at risk."

She'd figured it out. All of it. He had no defenses, no quick excuses, nothing. "You're right," he said hoarsely.

"I'm not finished." She walked around the desk until she was standing next to him. "I love you, Jim Dyer. Knowing all that I know, knowing the best you are or the worst you can be, I love you."

He jerked as if he'd been struck, his mind and body recoiling to reject her words. "You can't."

"I can, and I do. I love you. Even when you're distant. Even when you're hiding from me. I love you. I'll keep saying it until you believe it. And I'm going to fight to keep you."

She handed Diane to him. The familiar soft, warm weight felt so right in his arms. Diane grinned as she looked up at him and waved her arms. He'd missed them both so much the pain of it nearly overwhelmed him.

"Hey, sweet cheeks," he murmured.

"Now comes *my* confession," Heather said.

He looked up startled. "What?"

Color stained her face. "I don't want to just be friends, Jim. I want it all. You're the only father Diane has ever known. She loves you and I believe you love her, too. You're not perfect, but you're perfect for us, and we're right for you, too. We belong together and we can have a wonderful life together if only you'll give us a chance. I know your deepest, darkest secret and it doesn't disgust me or scare me. It makes me love you more. I know that there will always be some things you can't fix and guess what? That's okay. I still love you, and I'm not leaving. I'll be right here underfoot, loving you and showing you that it's safe to love me, too."

With that, she turned on her heel and walked over to her desk. She sat down and started working as if the conversation had never taken place.

Jim continued to ignore Heather for the next four days. Which was not to say she ignored him. She spoke to him, teased him, told him jokes and touched him. In a way, the touching was the worst. Little brushes of her fingers against his arms, a light caress on the back of his neck, and once, in the lunchroom, a full body press by the refrigerator. She was killing him slowly.

He couldn't breathe without thinking of her. Work had been reduced to either being with Heather, or not. His only relief came when he played with Diane, but being with her was its own special kind of torture. Because she had pretty blue eyes and a direct gaze just like her mother. And her eyes filled with the same emotion—the one emotion he was terrified to want—love.

He leaned against the window frame and stared out toward the hangar. A warm Santa Ana wind was blowing across the airport and Brian had brought in a kite. Heather and the teenager crouched beside Diane's stroller while the baby clapped her hands in delight at the brightly colored diamond of fabric floating up in the air.

"At the risk of repeating myself," Flo said, walking toward him, "how long are you going to be stupid? And don't tell me you don't know. I need a better answer than that."

Jim wished he had one. "I don't know what she wants from me."

"Of course you do. She wants what most other people want. She wants a man she can love and respect, who will love and respect her in return. She wants to get married and have more babies. She wants to be happy."

Flo's words painted a picture that was a fantasy— something he could never give Heather.

"It wouldn't work."

"Why not?"

"I can't—"

He found himself being physically turned until he faced Flo. She stared up at him, her eyes blazing with anger, her fingers digging into his arms. "I'm so sick of this," she said, practically yelling at him. "I don't know what happened in your past, but I'm willing to bet it was horrible. And I have just one thing to say about that. *So what?* We all have bad things in our past. You think I liked being a punching bag for all those years? Do you think I'm proud of how long I put up with it? Well, I'm not. But I've made peace with my past and moved on. It's time for you to do

the same. Let it go, Jim. Isn't that what you tell people who come to work here? That their pasts don't
matter, that they're starting fresh today? Give yourself
the same break. You are being given the most wonderful opportunity of your life, and if you're not careful, you're going to lose it. Women like Heather don't
come along every day.''

She didn't know what she was asking. ''I've spent
the past twenty years learning how *not* to need anyone
or let anyone get close.''

''So? Unlearn it.'' She shoved his shoulder until he
was facing the window again. ''Do you see that? You
could have that. All you have to do is admit you love
her. You do, you know. You have since the moment
you met her. Just take one small chance. I promise
you won't regret it.''

He heard her walk away, but he didn't move from
his place at the window. He stared at the family scene
in front of him and felt a longing so strong he thought
he might die. His entire life history told him she
couldn't possibly love him. That somehow even if she
did, he would fail her. But he wasn't sure he was
strong enough to let her walk away.

A gust of wind sent the kite crashing into the
ground. He watched as Heather spoke with the teenager, then headed back to the office. Jim quickly took
his seat.

Suddenly, Heather walked into the office and
paused. ''Where's Flo?'' she asked. ''I have to leave
for a dentist appointment and she said she would
watch Diane.''

Heather was wearing a pink dress with short
sleeves and buttons down the front. Soft blond curls

teased at her face. She was tall and slender and the most beautiful woman he'd ever seen.

"I can watch her," he said, a little surprised that he could talk.

She didn't look convinced. "Maybe she's in back."

"I think she left, but I don't know where she went."

Heather frowned. "How odd. That's not like her at all. We just talked about it earlier this morning. I don't think she forgot."

"Don't worry. Diane and I will be fine."

He stood up and walked around to take the baby out of her stroller. Diane grinned when she saw him. He picked her up and kissed her cheek. At least being with Diane would help him forget about Heather for a little while.

"I don't really have a choice," she said. "Not that I don't appreciate this, but I'm a little worried about Flo. Are you sure you'll be all right? I could take her with me."

Are you sure you'll be all right?

He understood how she meant the question, but suddenly those seven words took on a significance far greater than what she'd implied. Would he be all right? He looked at the baby smiling up at him, at that baby's lovely mother. He thought about all the joy they'd brought to him. How he only felt complete and healed when he was with Heather. He thought about the shared laughter and how she understood that it was important for him to help people. He thought about how she'd seen into the withered darkness of his soul and still claimed to love him.

No, not claimed. He knew Heather well enough to

know that she didn't say things she didn't mean. She loved him. Who was he trying to kid? There was no way he could live without these two in his life. He couldn't stand to be alone anymore. He had to let her inside. He had to love her and let her love him back.

Heather shifted her handbag onto her shoulder. "I guess I'll be going."

He took a step toward her. "No. Don't go. Please. I want..." He paused, not sure what he needed to say. Then he realized the truth would be the easiest. "I love you."

Her eyes opened wide. "What?"

"I love you. I need you so much. I can't breathe without you. You are the light of my world, and so is your daughter. I don't want you to take another job and I don't want you to walk out of my life. I don't want Diane to know a father other than me." He took another step closer until he could have touched her.

He shifted the baby so she rested in the crook of his right arm, and with his left, he pulled Heather close. "I thought if I kept rescuing everyone else, no one would notice that I was the one nearly drowning. But you saw that."

"Oh, Jim." She rested her forehead against his shoulder.

"I love you, and I want to marry you. I want us to be a real family. I want us to have more kids and to always be together. I'll do anything. Just please don't go."

She raised her head and he saw tears glimmering in her eyes. "I could never leave you." She smiled. "Even when you were too stubborn to realize we belonged together." Her smile faded. "Are you scared?"

"Terrified. But I'm going to risk it all because I don't want to lose you."

"You won't." She kissed him. "You can't."

"You can't lose me, either." He touched her face, then cupped the back of her neck and drew her to him. "Let me love you forever."

"Only if you let me love you right back."

He agreed, because now there weren't any doubts. As she held him close and murmured how much she cared, he felt the last shard of pain fall from his heart and blow away. The past would always be a part of him because it had shaped who he had become. But it no longer owned him. He'd found a different place to live. He'd finally found where he belonged...right in Heather's arms.

* * * * *

*Don't miss the next exciting
Susan Mallery project!
Look for a special 2-in-1 Special Edition—*

A MONTANA MAVERICK'S CHRISTMAS,

*featuring MARRIED IN WHITEHORN,
a short story by Susan Mallery*

*and BORN IN WHITEHORN,
a short story by Karen Hughes...*

*only from Silhouette Special Edition,
December 1999*

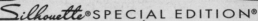

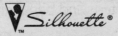

Don't miss Silhouette's newest cross-line promotion,

Four royal sisters find their own Prince Charmings as they embark on separate journeys to find their missing brother, the Crown Prince!

Royally Wed

The search begins in October 1999 and continues through February 2000:

On sale October 1999: **A ROYAL BABY ON THE WAY** by award-winning author **Susan Mallery** (Special Edition)

On sale November 1999: **UNDERCOVER PRINCESS** by bestselling author **Suzanne Brockmann** (Intimate Moments)

On sale December 1999: **THE PRINCESS'S WHITE KNIGHT** by popular author **Carla Cassidy** (Romance)

On sale January 2000: **THE PREGNANT PRINCESS** by rising star **Anne Marie Winston** (Desire)

On sale February 2000: **MAN...MERCENARY...MONARCH** by top-notch talent **Joan Elliott Pickart** (Special Edition)

ROYALLY WED
Only in—
SILHOUETTE BOOKS

Available at your favorite retail outlet.

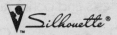
Silhouette®

Visit us at www.romance.net

SSERW

THE FORTUNES OF TEXAS

*Membership in this family has
its privileges…and its price.
But what a fortune can't buy,
a true-bred Texas love is sure to bring!*

Coming in November 1999…

Expecting…
In Texas
by

MARIE
FERRARELLA

Wrangler Cruz Perez's night of passion with Savannah Clark
had left the beauty pregnant with his child. Cruz's cowboy
code of honor demanded he do right by the expectant
mother, but could he convince Savannah—and himself—
that his offer of marriage was inspired by true love?

THE FORTUNES OF TEXAS continues with
A Willing Wife by Jackie Merritt,
available in December 1999 from
Silhouette Books.

Available at your favorite retail outlet.

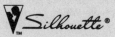

Silhouette®

#1279 THE NO-NONSENSE NANNY—Penny Richards
That Special Woman!
When pampered heiress Amber Campion took on the job of temporary
nanny, she soon realized she was in way over her head. But somehow the
kids' devoted uncle Cal always managed to soothe her frazzled nerves.
She'd foolishly walked away from the sexy sheriff once, but *twice?* Not on
her life!

#1280 CINDERELLA'S BIG SKY GROOM—Christine Rimmer
Montana Mavericks: Return to Whitehorn
Lynn Taylor's fantasy-filled date with Ross Garrison was a fairy tale come
true—until the Whitehorn gossips got wind of their "affair." To save face,
the virginal beauty reluctantly agreed to a pretend engagement to her
dashing Prince Charming. But could they live happily-ever-after for *real?*

#1281 A ROYAL BABY ON THE WAY—Susan Mallery
Royally Wed
Against his better judgment, levelheaded rancher Mitch Colton agreed to
help beguiling Princess Alexandra of Wynborough find her missing brother.
But he never dreamed that their smoldering attraction would result in a royal
baby-to-be....

#1282 YOURS FOR NINETY DAYS—Barbara McMahon
Ellie Winslow thought she'd seen it *all* since opening her halfway house for
troubled teens. Everything changed when mysterious Nick Tanner became a
part of her makeshift family. Her rational side cautioned that the hard-edged
stranger was off-limits, but her heart wasn't listening....

#1283 PREGNANT & PRACTICALLY MARRIED—Andrea Edwards
The Bridal Circle
When rodeo cowboy Jed McCarron's heroics led the whole town to believe
he was betrothed to pregnant doc Karin Spencer, he found himself playing
the part of adoring fiancé—and doting daddy-to-be—a little *too* well.

#1284 COWBOY BOOTS AND GLASS SLIPPERS—Jodi O'Donnell
Although she was dubbed a modern-day Cinderella, suddenly single
Lacey McCoy vowed to shed the regal typecast. Trouble was, no one back
home believed her—especially Will Proffitt, who insisted the slipper still fit.
So she set out to prove to the sexiest cowboy in the Lone Star State how
wrong he was!